The Murder In Manilla

Bob Able

Copyright © 2026 Bob Able

All rights reserved

The characters and events portrayed in this book are fictitious. Any similarity to real persons, living or dead, is coincidental and not intended by the author.

No part of this book may be reproduced, stored in a retrieval system, or transmitted in any form or by any means, electronic, mechanical, photocopying, recording, or otherwise, without the express written permission of the author.

Cover photo: John Mark Strange

The Murder In Manilla

Bob Able

INTRODUCTION

September.

Sweeping the raindrops off the clear cover of the 'Armpocket' pouch on her upper arm, she checked the time on her mobile phone.

She had only been out twenty minutes, and this rain wasn't forecast.

The downpour was so sudden and so forceful that running through it was quite painful. That was why she had stopped to catch her breath on the raised concrete path, beside the row of gaily painted beach huts.

There was no shelter to be had there, but at least the stinging rain wasn't lashing into her eyes.

She looked around and listened.

This early, nobody was about as usual, and the beach was deserted. The only sound was the endless suck and slop of the waves on the stony beach and the hissing of the rain as it hit the water.

The sky, which had merely been overcast when she set out for her run, was now black and threatening, and any trace of the early light of dawn had been dimmed down to a watery glow.

She turned to look at the beach huts beside her.

Locked up now, to await the new season, their carnival colours presented an odd contrast to the grey sky. In places, she noticed, the wood was rotting, and several of the little structures would need a spruce up before they were occupied again. She knew that they were leased by the same families year after year in the summer, but the holidaymakers were all gone now.

Each, she noticed, had a number, and most had been personalised with the addition of name plates, in a motley collection of styles, screwed or nailed to the wooden walls or the doors.

Looking left and right, she read "Florida", "Sunny Nook", "The Cabin", "Miami", and the rather more practical "Joe's Hut".

And then three doors along from where she stood, one called "Manilla". She did a double-take. That was a spelling mistake, surely, Manila only had one 'l'?

However, the brightly painted door of the hut called 'Manilla' was very slightly ajar.

She walked along to stand outside the hut, thinking that here, perhaps, was a kindly soul who might offer her shelter from the downpour.

Her polite cough drew no response, and neither did her slightly louder 'Hello?', so she knocked on the door. It had obviously swollen and was binding on the frame, but it opened up a little bit more after she gave it a push.

Maybe she could just step inside for a moment, until the worst of the rain abated.

'Hello?' she called again, 'Anyone home?'

No response, so she gave the door another more determined push, and this time it swung open.

The interior of the little building was quite dark, but she could see at a glance that there was nobody in residence.

There was the obligatory kettle, a small gas ring on a shelf, and beside two deckchairs, one of those folding 'Z-beds' standing against the wall by the door. But there was also something else.

Partly covered by a threadbare rug in the middle of

the tiny space was what, at first, she took to be a heap of old clothes.

Without meaning to, or for that matter being invited, she had stepped into the hut, and now that her eyes had adjusted to the gloom, she could see more clearly.

The heap of old clothes had an ankle and a foot, encased in a tatty trainer, protruding from one end.

Emma felt the bile rising in her throat.

She had failed to scream, which might have helped, and only emitted a sort of strangled squeak. But there was no denying what her eyes told her. There was a dead body on the floor.

It was partly covered by a once-floral, threadbare rug, and pushing a corner up with her running shoe, Emma had revealed the face, with a gaping mouth locked in a rictus of terror, and bulging sightless eyes that seemed to follow her as she stepped back in horror.

She reached for her phone and tugged at the velcro securing it within the pouch on her upper arm. She would call the police.

But, before she could wrestle the phone from its hiding place, she was suddenly unable to help herself. She turned, stepped out of the beach hut and vomited violently on the rain-soaked walkway.

THE MURDER IN MANILLA

***

Chapter 1

Elliot Markham was a naturally cheerful soul, and that appealed to the customers of his business.

'Elliots Estate Agents' was formed by his father shortly after he was born, and following that great pillar of the local society's demise, was now owned and run by Elliot himself. If an estate agency might never actually aspire to be liked, it was at least respected as part of the street furniture in the busy little seaside town.

Elliot knew his job too and dealt with incomers and the mostly retired residents of the town confidently. He had earned some personal popularity by following in his father's footsteps as an enthusiastic sponsor of the local cricket club, and was a regular attendee at the meetings of the thriving 'Round Table'. And, although far from proficient at the game, he also maintained his membership of the links golf club and was on the committee of the 'Flower Show and Fete', held every year on the recreation ground.

With twin boys in the local primary school, and a pretty wife who was content to be kept busy with charity work when not making the 'cricket teas' in due season, or helping out in the office by folding and stuffing manila envelopes with property details to mail out, life for Elliot was going well.

Since employing Emma Johnson, and a few years after promoting her to her current position as 'Senior Negotiator', Elliot could also let the business run itself if the opportunity for a game of golf arose, or during their annual family holiday in the little house in France his father had left him.

As Elliot told anyone who would listen, he was indeed a very lucky man.

***

Panda had always been called Panda.

It was her little brother's fault. When he was very small, getting his tongue around 'Amanda' had proved beyond him, so he had called her Panda, and it had stuck.

She met Elliot as a result of her efforts with the local amateur dramatic society, which he briefly joined. Now they had been married almost twelve years, and with their two boisterous boys to care for, Panda always seemed to be busy.

If she wasn't helping out at the estate agent's office, she was involved in something at the school or the cricket club, or, when time allowed, helping out at the charity shop, which she always enjoyed.

Now, as the rain lashed against the kitchen windows and on the tall French doors in the bay, she sat with her coffee at the big scrubbed wood table and sighed.

She always loved this time in the early morning, before the boys got up and all the usual chaos erupted, as she struggled to get them ready for school. But sometimes, as would be the case today, she would be assisted by her husband, who, as it was raining, had offered to take them to school in the Range Rover.

Panda hated rain, and for her, the opportunity not to have to go out in it was wonderful.

She stood up and walked over to the doors and watched the water streaming down the glass, distorting the view down the wide, meandering garden path that led to the sea, and the narrow path at the top of the cliffs.

Because of the slope, from her position, she could not see the top of the wall at the bottom of the garden or the tall gate which led to the clifftop path beyond. From here, it appeared that the garden rolled uninterrupted right to the edge of the steep cliff.

The brick path was wide enough for the gardener to drive his old truck full of lawnmowers right down the steep slope and park on the concrete base of a long-removed shed beside the tall wall when he visited and worked on the area at the bottom of the garden. There would be no gardener today, however, not in this weather.

'Let it rain,' she thought. 'I might even treat myself to a long soak in the bath when the boys have gone.'

***

Elliot sat on the side of the bed and tried to compose himself.

After Emma and her friends left the golf club bar to go off for a meal, he had stayed on with the chaps, and if he was honest with himself, he had a bit too much to drink. Or perhaps, he thought, there was something off in the leftover remains of the buffet lunch that they helped themselves to.

They were there, after work, to kick off the celebrations for Emma's fortieth birthday, and she had arranged for her girlfriends to meet up at the golf club for an early drink and leave their cars there while they walked into town.

The charity golf society who had been there earlier in the day had done themselves proud, but left quite a bit of their buffet lunch spread out on the table at one end of the bar, and after Emma and her friends left, the chaps had begun to help themselves to soak up the booze as the evening wore on, before the kitchen staff got round to clearing it away.

Elliot had made a bit of a pig of himself with those scotch eggs and the tandoori chicken wings, and now he was regretting it.

'Panda,' he called down the stairs. 'I'm not feeling too well, and I've got a rotten gut ache. Have we got any Alka-Seltzer?'

***

The police were taking their time and wouldn't let Emma leave the 'scene of the crime' until they had satisfied themselves that they had examined every corner of the beach hut and the surrounding area.

Mercifully, the rain had stopped, but Emma, in her running gear, was getting cold, and she was worried that she would be late for work.

Today, of all days, she did not want to be late for work.

Elliot was itching to tease her, she knew, and if she was even a minute late, he would go on and on about her birthday and overdoing the celebrations. Not that anything like that was likely, as Emma gave up alcohol several years ago. But that wouldn't stop

Elliot.

He was a sweetie, really, although sometimes he could be a bit childish. Probably, she thought, because he had led something of a sheltered life. A bit spoilt, maybe. Straight out of college and into the family business, and living in the admittedly lovely big old house where he grew up, with his boys and Panda.

She smiled to herself as she thought that Panda pandered to his every need. But she shouldn't be uncharitable. Panda was generally delightful and came from a wealthy local farming family. She was the only daughter of Sir Lemuel Fulton-Marks and went to a very posh school. And it showed. She was always elegant and stylish. Everything that Emma aspired to be, but could never achieve. Emma wouldn't have married Elliot, but she might at least have managed to marry *someone* if she looked like that.

As she waited about for the police to say she could go, and sitting on a folding chair, positioned on the walkway just along from where she had been sick, Emma had nothing to do except chew the mint gum the kindly young policewoman had offered her to clear her mouth, and let her mind wander.

As the shock of discovering the body had receded, and following a cursory check over by one of the ambulance men who had arrived and had produced the folding chair, she felt a little surplus to requirements and asked yet again if she could go now.

'We need to ask you to hang on a bit, I'm afraid,' said the policeman. 'A detective is coming down, and he might want to hear what happened from you. He should be here any second. If you are getting cold, I could get you another one of those space blanket things if you like.'

Emma pulled the shiny, crinkly silver blanket a little tighter around her shoulders, but declined the offer. The policeman had enough to do without worrying about her.

***

Detective Sergeant Mark Curtis read Emma's statement in the lady Police Constable's notebook and nodded.

'Nice handwriting, Linda,' he commented as he handed the notebook back. 'I wish everyone, including myself, could write as clearly as that.'

Turning to face Emma, now standing beside the folding chair, he said something to the effect that he did not think they needed to detain her further, and almost before the words were out of his mouth, Emma was off, sprinting for the steep walkway that led to the top of the cliffs, thirty metres above them, and a quick hot shower.

While she waited, she had been told that the police may need to interview her again, and asked twice whether she knew the deceased, who it emerged was a local fisherman. She had made a statement and given her name and address before being reminded not to talk to the press, but she had to wait until the detective arrived to be told that she could go.

If she really hurried, she could still get to the office in time.

***

'Perhaps he had a key to the beach hut,' offered DS Curtis, making himself more comfortable on the hard interview room chair back at the police station. 'There are no signs of a forced entry and no indication that the body was dragged there. And as you saw, the door was on the latch.'

'So it might be reasonable to assume that he died there,' said Detective Inspector Paul Francis, looking again at the report in front of him.

'Yes, and from the look of it, as the result of one of two deep stab wounds to the chest,' added DS Curtis.

'Not much blood in evidence,' DI Francis observed, examining the crime scene photographs again.

'No. I expect forensics will say that is because he

was on his back and most of it was retained in the body through postmortem hypostasis,' speculated DS Curtis.

'Postmortem what?'

'Hypostasis, sir. When the heart stops pumping the blood around, gravity draws it to the lowest part of the body. It pools in the little capillaries and clots there. If you ask me, one of those stab wounds went upwards, straight into his heart through his lung. I bet they find the blood there.'

'You might be right, Curtis, but until the scientists have had a look at him, we can't know for certain.'

'Of course not, sir. I only thought to mention ...'

'Yes, well, fair enough. I hope nobody has touched the door, there might be fingerprints ... Still no sign of the murder weapon, I assume?' DS Curtis shook his head. 'So the big issue for us is to try to understand why anyone would want to kill an old local fisherman who, by all accounts, had very little money and not many friends. Have we managed to get an interview with his son yet?'

'He moved to London some years ago, sir, and we are still trying to track him down.'

'What about any business contacts. Did he work with anyone else?'

'He worked alone, as far as we can establish, and other than a bit of rivalry with one of the other fishing families down there, who had tried to buy him out several times, there is not much to go on.'

'This other family tried to buy him out?'

'Don't get too concerned about that, sir. The Richards family have tried to buy out every single fishing boat with crabbing rights all along this coast at one time or another. They have an idea to increase their hold on the market, and to a greater or lesser degree, have been gathering up further fishing rights for years. The local fishermen know all about it and even refer to it as their "retirement plan"!'

'No threats applied then?'

'Oh, plenty of threats and the occasional punch up, mostly in the pub, but the family is largely harmless, and the fishermen all know where they stand with them.'

'Presumably ...'

'Yes, sir. Interviews are already underway.'

'Who owns the beach hut?'

'We are looking into that, sir. Someone is due to interview the managing agent this afternoon.'

***

Andrew Gurney curled into a tight ball and pulled the quilt over his head as he tried to ignore the telephone ringing insistently in the next room.

This was the third time it had rung, and it wasn't even ten o'clock.

Everyone he knew was aware that he never got out of bed before ten o'clock. So that might mean it was someone he didn't know.

People he didn't know startled Andrew, and although he lived in London, surrounded by thousands of such people, he had taught himself to tune them out. The ability to do that was one of the advantages of his condition.

Telephones were different, though. They were no respecters of anyone's desire for privacy, and usually, since the occasion when the damn thing rang when they were making love, he left it off the hook.

As it stopped ringing at last, he was reminded of that occasion again, and it opened an old wound. Andrew was shy. Painfully shy. And while he could express himself boldly, even aggressively, through his painting, he knew he was not much good at real people.

Since Guy from the gallery had convinced him to move up to London to share his flat several years ago, when his work started to sell, he had not been able to connect with people. Or beforehand, come to think about it.

But there had been that one time. That really special time. And the damn telephone had ruined it.

Overall, the move to London had been a success, however.

Andrew's parents were simple folk who had no idea how to cope with their talented but withdrawn son. They did their best, but when his mother died, things started to fall apart. It didn't help that he was so terribly frightened of the sea.

If he had been one of those robust boys from his school, or had been able to believe all the stuff his mother and her church tried to get him to accept, he would probably be out on the boat with his father even now. But he just couldn't do it.

To start with, his mother protected him when his father tried to tempt, cajole and encourage him to get involved in fishing. But then, as he got older, the talk turned to 'duty', and his father's frustration turned to shouting. Then, just once, the threat, never carried through, of a raised hand. After that, things changed as his father had to force himself to back off. He had to accept that Andrew would never take over the boat, and that he himself would be the last of a long line of fishermen in his family.

Now, Andrew made more money from the sale of just one of his paintings than his father could make in a year, or even two, but for his father, that was not the point. There had been Gurneys fishing those same waters for hundreds of years, and Andrew was his only son, as he repeatedly said.

There wasn't really a rift between the two of them, but after Andrew moved to London with Guy, who had taken on a job in a West End gallery, contact became increasingly sporadic. Eventually, however, a routine was developed, and every three months they wrote to each other, and of course Christmas and birthday cards were exchanged, but that was about all.

His father's letters generally asked practical things, like whether he was eating properly, although there was always one consistent theme. Each time he wrote, his father asked about Andrew's money and what he was doing with it, and each time he simply replied that Guy handled all that, so he didn't have to worry about it.

Andrew was startled out of his thoughts, as now there was a knock at the door.

***

'It seems Sir Lemuel Fulton-Marks owns all those beach huts, sir,' said DS Curtis. 'The agent manages them and lets 'em out each summer. But they won't tell us who leased that one because of data protection.'

'Does he now. Well, we had better pay the Noble Lord a respectful call and see if we can't convince him to get the agent to tell us who he rented that one to.'

Chapter 2

Today, after dropping the twins off at school, Panda had a job to do.

She had called in at the estate agency and picked up a box of freshly photocopied property particulars and a bigger box of brown manila envelopes. At home, she fired up the computer and the printer in Elliot's study and loaded the latter with ready-made blank sticky address labels on A4-size sheets.

Her job was to open a database containing names and addresses of people searching for property who had registered with the agency and print off address labels.

Then she folded the property particulars and a covering letter, and put each in a thin brown envelope, which had the gummed flap on the short side, and attached an address label.

The agency chose these brown envelopes in particular, not because they were cheap, although they undoubtedly were, but because with the flap on one of the short sides, it was easier to push in the folded property particulars. As these mailings were sometimes several sheets of paper thick, this design avoided splitting the envelope. Experience had shown that they also stood up well to the rigours of the postal system, and mostly arrived at their destination intact.

The only problem with them, as Panda and the staff often complained, was that the gum applied to the flap tasted horrible, so now they used a glue stick.

When it was done, on each occasion she would pack the filled envelopes in the cardboard boxes and take them to the Post Office to be franked, and once she had signed the invoice for the postage costs, they would be sent on to the hopefully eager property hunters.

'Mail Out Day', as they called it, was a slightly old-fashioned way of doing things and quite time-consuming, but Elliots had to deal with many people of, or beyond, retirement age, who might struggle with emails and computers. This showed them an element of courtesy often missing in the cut and thrust of modern estate agency. And each time they asked, they received assurances that getting paper copies of the property particulars was appreciated.

Panda liked doing it too, and very occasionally she would sneak in personal letters to her friends in the manila envelopes, and take them to be franked at the company's expense. She knew it was cheeky, but when you looked at the size of the postal bill the agency ran up, she didn't really think anyone was likely to notice, or mind too much. She was the boss's wife after all.

***

'It must have been awful,' said Karen, who was fairly recently appointed, straight from school, as an office junior. 'I'd of been off for a week with stress, like, if I saw a dead body!'

'Yes, I imagine you would,' said Emma. 'But it is no good thinking like that or giving in to things, Karen.'

'Did you see the knife what done him? Was it one of those zombie knives?'

'I know I sound like an old fogey, but one really does have to grow a thicker skin as one goes through life, and just get on with it, you know. And no, I didn't see the knife, it was bad enough just coming across the body, and I didn't want to look too closely.'

'Thick skin? Like when my granny had thickening of the toenails? The nurse at the doctor's had to cut them back. And you're not an old fogey yet, Emma, even though you are like forty.'

'That is not quite what I meant, Karen, but never mind. How about making us a nice cup of tea?'

***

'Elliot? It's your father-in-law here.'

'Oh, hello,' Elliot noticed a touch of annoyance in Sir Lemuel's voice.

'Look here, I've got a house full of plod here who claim you are being uncooperative about giving them the name of someone who rented a ruddy beach hut. Why won't you tell 'em, boy?'

'Ah, yes. They have been here asking my staff about that,' said Elliot. 'And as a result, I looked up the records. The fact is that particular beach hut hasn't been rented out all summer. Nobody has been using it as far as we know.'

'What!' exploded Sir Lemuel. 'Well, some bugger got in there and died on the ruddy floor, and these detectives say the lock wasn't forced. So what do you make of that?'

'I really have no idea,' stuttered Elliot. 'All the keys are carefully logged in and out, and there is no record of that one being used.'

'Where is the ruddy key now?'

'There are two keys, actually, both are hanging in their place on the hook.'

'I suppose you have got the right hut?'

'Absolutely. Those keys have not been logged out all year.'

There was a pause in the conversation while Sir Lemuel discussed this revelation with the detectives.

'All right, Elliot, my boy. Stand down. The rozzers say they might pop in and borrow the keys, but for now, don't worry about it.'

'Well, hang on, there is just one thing. At the end of every season, we clean up the huts, and last week Panda did it with Karen from the office, so if they are looking for fingerprints, that is what they might find.'

'Ah. Good point. I'll pass that on.'

***

Andrew sat on the sofa, and given the circumstances, allowed Guy to gently put his arm around his shoulders.

'So as I said, I'm very sorry to have to bring you this news about your father,' said the policeman. 'Is there anyone you would like us to contact, or is there someone who can look after you?'

It was very different last time.

Last month, on "mail-out day," before she went to the post office, Panda had to go into the offices of the Building Society and withdraw almost all the remaining money in the savings account she had kept adding to since she was a small girl.

Still using one of the estate agent's dull manila envelopes, this time addressed to a Post Office box number, she had sealed the money in, along with a pink Post-it note, on which she scrawled the words, "This is the last time, understand? I don't have access to any more money!"

On that occasion, as on each of the preceding ones, that particular letter needed to be posted separately, using a stamp.

Panda was relieved that she had heard no more from the recipient of the money this month and allowed herself to hope and believe that it really was finished at last.

***

After some discussion, following the policemen's visit, Andrew had made it clear that he did not need anyone to stay with him, so reluctantly Guy had gone back to work at the gallery.

Before he left, Guy had agreed to phone the flat at four o'clock to make sure he was OK. He knew from experience that it had to be exactly four o'clock, not five minutes early, or late, and he wrote himself a reminder on a Post-it note and stuck it on his desk when he got to the gallery.

Living with Andrew had its moments, but there was plenty of room in the vast converted Victorian flat for his studio, and it did mean that he could keep a close eye on the prodigy he had discovered. Guy's social life was suffering, but since his liaisons with the woman he was seeing were few and far between and had to be clandestine snatched moments, that didn't matter too much. The important thing was that the arrangement kept Andrew calm, and that, in turn, kept him painting.

Acting as his agent, Guy had made quite a lot of money out of Andrew's spectacular work, and he hoped that they could go on to make much more together.

Andrew's quiet life was carefully preserved and managed, and apart from the therapy sessions he attended twice weekly, just over the road, he rarely left the flat.

They had tried having supermarket food deliveries to save Guy time with the shopping, but on a couple of occasions, Andrew had refused to open the door, and finding delivery 'slots' in the evening or at weekends, when he was at home, was very difficult. So each week Guy did all their shopping on his way back to the flat. He did all the cooking and also cleaned, following an incident when the cleaning company sent out a different operative, and Andrew shut himself in his bedroom and refused to let her in.

Apart from the recent sale of another painting, there had been one bright spot in Guy's otherwise regimented life in recent months. On that occasion, Panda had been invited to a school reunion, somewhere near Knightsbridge, and when Andrew went off to his therapy session, she came to the flat.

They made love fast, desperate for release, and then more slowly. But unfortunately, wrapped up in each other, they lost track of time. Were it not for the telephone ringing, they might not have noticed that Andrew had returned and was sitting on the end of the sofa watching them through the open bedroom door.

Andrew's condition meant that he had no 'filter' and was not aware that he was doing anything wrong or was likely to cause embarrassment. He knew who Panda was, of course, as she came from his hometown, but he openly stared in fascination at her nakedness as she rushed to the bathroom.

Afterwards, and at last with a mental picture of a naked woman in his head, Andrew had tried to draw the scene. But he had always struggled to draw people, and they rarely featured in his work except as blurred shapes in the background. As a result, he became frustrated and did not find his initial sketches satisfactory.

Eventually, he had torn them up and returned to safer ground in his studio, where he continued to work on a panel of the panorama of the River Thames at Westminster, and the incident was not mentioned again.

***

Karen, in the office, had known Mikey, the window cleaner, all her life.

Each time he came around to clean the estate agent's windows, she had a cup of coffee waiting for him and took time for a chat.

'Bad business, that,' he said. 'Old Stan Gurney kept himself to himself, like, but he was a harmless old soul, I thought. Been crabbing here as long as I can remember.'

'I was saying to Emma, it must have been dreadful finding the actual body, like. I dunno what I'd of done if it was me …'

'I 'spect you would've passed out, or had a hissy fit like you used to in the shop when your mum wouldn't buy you no sweets.'

'Oh shut up, Mikey! That was years ago. I'm like all grown up now!'

'Yus, you are, girl,' said Mikey, allowing his eyes to rove over her pneumatic chest. 'Yus you are.'

'Oh shut up, Mikey, you old letch!' squeaked Karen, blushing deeply, and attempting to cover her chest with her arm, but still smiling. 'Shut up!'

Later on, when he got back to the flat over his mother's sweet shop, where he still lived, Mikey would try again to find the words to ask Karen out, and would write them down on a slip of paper to put in his pocket to learn by heart as he went on his rounds. This time, he was finally going to overcome his nerves and do it, he told himself.

***

At lunchtime, Elliot found Emma sitting on one of the benches by the church, staring blankly ahead of her. Her untouched sandwich and energy drink sat on the bench by her side.

'You all right, Emma?' he asked.

She had not noticed his approach and shook herself

as she looked up at him.

'Sorry, Elliot. I'll be back at the office in a minute. I just …'

'Take all the time you need, Emma. I'm surprised you are even at work after what you saw.'

'Thank you, Elliot. I'll be alright in a minute.'

'Here,' said Elliot, 'I've got a clean hanky. You might like to dry your eyes.'

Emma had not even realised she had been crying.

Chapter 4

Betty Richards bore a strong resemblance to all of her family, even the men.

She had brawny arms and a slightly intimidating physique, and behind her large, thick, round glasses, her eyes were so close together that the thin bridge of her nose barely separated them.

'What do you want?' she enquired rudely as she opened the door to DS Curtis and Linda Pope, the young WPC.

After the reason for their visit had been explained, she asked if the police officers knew Andrew Gurney's address in London, but they explained that they were not allowed to pass on those details.

'I only want to express me sympathies,' she explained.

'Or try to convince Andrew to give you an option to purchase his father's crabbing licence when it passes to him, perhaps, Betty?'

'There is a time and a place …' coughed Betty, doing her best impression of looking mortified. 'Anyway, I suppose the Burrows will be all over him once the papers get a hold of it. I don't deny we want his licence, but the Burrows have been hounding old Stan about it for years, and the old bugger never wanted to sell to *them*.'

'The Burrows,' explained DS Curtis, as they got back into the car, 'are the other big fishing family along this coast. They have been snapping at the Richards heels for years.'

'I guessed as much,' said Linda.

As the car drove away, Betty Richards had her mobile phone in her hand and was connecting to Google. If the local police would not divulge Andrew Gurney's whereabouts, she would bet that it would not take the Press long to dig him up. And in return for a juicy story or two about the Gurney family, she was sure they would cough up where he was.

***

When Guy Lombardi left his job at the fine art auctioneers in the sought-after upmarket town along the coast for a much more lucrative job in London, he had promised it would not be the end of his clandestine relationship with Panda.

Panda was not so sure. Guy had just sort of

happened to her. She hadn't meant it to go so far, but now she was in too deep to just walk away.

Panda had joined an eight-week art appreciation course being run at the local town hall, and Guy was there to assist the mercurial retired university professor who took the course. The auctioneer provided original artwork by local artists for them to examine, and huge printed facsimiles, which Guy pinned up on the walls, of some of the great paintings of the world, for the professor to eulogise over.

Guy cut a pretty impressive figure. Panda found out later that he was six foot four in his socks, under his mane of dark hair. He had a muscular and powerful build and a broad chest. He also dressed with some style and was so well versed in the art they were looking at that he could probably have run the course on his own.

Panda refused his first three offers of coffee or a drink after the lesson, but on the next occasion, heavy rain had started while they were inside the building, and it showed no sign of abating as they were leaving. Panda hated rain and had parked her car some distance away, so was persuaded to join Guy, and one or two others from the course, in the coffee bar two doors down.

The other course members had long since gone, and the rain had stopped by the time Panda made her way home.

Guy's knowledge, courteous ways, and, of course, his looks had entranced her, and for the remaining weeks of the program, she followed him to the cafe like a lamb as each of the sessions ended.

Subsequently, they met up when Elliot was at work, and before the boys came home from school, Guy came to the house initially to look at the fairly dull collection of old paintings Elliot's father had amassed. They did at least glance at some of the pictures before they found themselves in each other's arms.

Panda had not meant it to happen. She was a happily married woman, she told herself. And it was the truth, as far as it went. Guy just happened.

***

Emma didn't want to run by the beach huts again, but something drew her to them.

She had heard that the investigation into who killed Stanley Gurney had all but stalled, and since they had not found a murder weapon or any witnesses who might be able to point to a motive, the detectives were getting nowhere.

It was easy to spot the hut called 'Manilla'. The police had installed an enormous hasp and padlock across the door and stuck up a notice warning the public to keep away.

As she drew closer, Emma noticed something else different about the hut.

Pushed up into the eaves of the roof, and pointing down towards the door was a tiny CCTV camera, no bigger than her fist.

Emma remembered reading somewhere that sometimes criminals like to return to the scene of their crimes, and she wondered if identifying whoever it was, if they did come back, was why the camera had been installed.

With a sharp intake of breath, she realised that she was revisiting the scene of the crime herself, and she abruptly turned on her heel and ran back down the beach the other way.

***

Elliot opened the little metal locking cabinet on the wall of the windowless back room, where all the keys were hung up and safely stored.

There was not much value in a few beach huts, and the key safe contained keys for much more valuable properties, where the agency had been entrusted with them, to show prospective purchasers around, or to arrange handovers when properties were sold.

They only hung onto the contract to manage the

beach huts, and a few other properties which were rented out from time to time, near the sea or around the farm, as a favour to Sir Lemuel, who owned them. Or rather had inherited them as part of the estate where he and his family had lived for several generations.

Elliot made no money out of the arrangement, really, and it was actually a bit of a nuisance. But Sir Lemuel was his father-in-law, and the arrangement had gone on for years.

How, he wondered now, had anyone got into the beach hut in question without access to these keys, and apparently without breaking in.

Now that he came to think about it, the locks had been changed on all of the beach huts three or four years ago when some 'new age travellers' broke into some of them and tried to make themselves at home. Elliots had organised for contractors to carry out the repair work, and he was pretty certain that each of the new locks only had two keys.

He looked at the hooks where the beach hut keys were kept. Each had two keys, no more, and no less, and all were present and correct.

Elliot realised that the mystery would have to remain unsolved a little longer. He would be late for the boys 'nets' at the cricket club if he didn't get a move on.

Chapter 5

A few years ago, Andrew's father had been persuaded to put one of his son's paintings in for an evaluation at the auctioneers where Guy worked.
The company recognised his talent immediately and dispatched Guy to meet his father and discuss Andrew's particular social difficulties. And to see if a way could be found to entice the boy to sell some of his work.

Guy was surprised to find that Andrew was not hiding away in his bedroom at the cottage when he arrived, given what he had been told. But although the boy sat apart at the dining table by the open back door, while he and his father sat on the uncomfortable wooden chairs in the garden, as the conversation moved on to art appreciation, Andrew emerged and shyly joined in.

Guy was astonished at the boy's encyclopaedic knowledge of fine art and particularly the techniques of the old masters, learned just from internet searches and the secondhand books his mother had bought for him. Although his father quickly confessed that the conversation was well over his head, a connection had been made, and Guy was invited to visit the house again to look at some more of Andrew's work.

His father explained, during one of these visits, that although he was now turning seventeen, Andrew had never formed any real friendships, and his relationship with Guy was as close as the boy had ever come to actually trusting anyone.

The timing was lucky. Guy had decided to leave the auctioneers and been offered a new and exciting job in London at a well-respected fine art gallery. But he returned each weekend to spend some more time with Andrew and to watch him paint. That was something nobody else, not even his father, had ever been allowed to see.

Guy learned how Andrew's autism affected his daily life and the struggles his father was having in coping with him. But gradually, between the three of them, a plan was hatched to launch Andrew's career in London, with Guy as his protector, agent and to some extent, nursemaid.

The owners of the gallery, who had by this time examined the various pieces of work Guy bought back for them to see, were encouraging about the idea and helped Guy to find a scruffy but huge old flat just around the corner from the gallery, with a superbly lit room to use as a studio.

The idea was explained to Andrew, and at first, it seemed to be going nowhere. But after two visits to London, although the boy found the travelling quite traumatic, he was at last convinced. In fact, having seen the room which was to be his studio, with its tall, wide windows and view over a little park, he embraced the plan and was keen to progress it as soon as the arrangements could be finalised.

The chosen location also had the benefit of being within walking distance of the London consulting rooms of the doctor who had taken Andrew under his wing at the expensive special school he had attended.

In the years since, the gallery had sold a series of Andrew's paintings, had arranged press coverage before the sales, and even had an appearance on the local TV news. Although he did not enjoy the media exposure, overall, Andrew and everyone involved were delighted with how it all turned out.

Everyone except Panda.

***

'Right, so we will meet the team there,' said DS Curtis. 'We have the keys, and everything is in place now, in terms of paperwork.'

At last, almost twenty-four hours after the

discovery of the body, the police were going to forensically examine Stan Gurney's house with the aid of a team of expert technicians called in from the central 'hub'. The delay had been frustrating for DS Curtis and his team, but they were told by their superiors that it was due to a lack of available manpower and could not be avoided.

In contrast, however, the autopsy report was returned surprisingly rapidly, breaking all previous records.

Now that the report was to hand, they learned that the nerves and muscles in Gurney's heart had been severed when penetrated by a sharp implement, currently unidentified, which had been pushed up under his rib-cage, through his diaphragm and into his heart. It had killed him almost instantly.

The report noted there was a similar upward thrust in evidence, presumably by the same instrument, which had pierced the cavity around the lungs where a considerable amount of blood had pooled.

There was an observation that the implement used had a small profile, and when the weapon had been withdrawn, the narrow entry point hole it created self-closed to some extent. As the pressure of blood was redirected to the cavity, very little escaped from the cadaver. The murder weapon, whatever it was, appeared to be capable of deeply stabbing, rather than slashing, the victim.

The report also contained an observation that the weapon must have been extremely sharp, long, and not much more than pencil-thin to achieve such deep penetration. Even so, it must have been thrust in with considerable force, and it surmised that it was most likely assisted, for the fatal stabbing, by the body falling forward onto it, perhaps from a standing position.

Given that the body was found lying face up, it could have been that the victim rolled over, having just been mortally wounded by an attack from the front, which would have caused him to stagger back. He may have stepped backwards against the immediately adjacent wall of the beach hut, and the collision caused him to fall forward. That may have served to embed the weapon further, as his weight fell onto it.

Because of the thin profile of the blade, it concluded, it did not create enough natural suction to prevent it from being withdrawn following the stabbing, although it would still have needed some determination to remove it from the body. Whilst it was not possible to state which of the two wounds was inflicted first, the non-fatal stab was less penetrative, indicating that it was not assisted by the effects of his weight if the victim fell onto it.

WPC Linda Pope shuddered as she read the gruesome report for a second time, and she wondered what sort of a knife, if indeed it could be described as a knife, could inflict such almost surgical wounds. Perhaps, she thought, it might have been a sword.

***

Panda scrolled through her messages.

If she was sure that it really had stopped now, perhaps she should delete the awful and frightening text messages she had been so terrified to open each time they arrived, over the last eight months. It would be difficult to explain if Elliot discovered them on her phone, and with 'No caller ID' displayed by each one, they did rather stand out amongst her other messages.

She thought the only other messages she had ever received which had 'No caller ID' were from the doctor or the gynaecologist, or that sort of thing. She didn't even know that you could turn off your 'caller ID' to text anonymously, but here was the evidence, and if you knew how, it seemed you could.

Except that it certainly wasn't the doctor's surgery, she had no idea who had sent the vile messages. All she had been able to do when they arrived each month was react and follow the instructions, the very expensive instructions, each message contained, or face the consequences. Those consequences would mean the end of her comfortable life with Elliot and her boys.

She wondered how this person, whoever it was, had got her number, but quickly realised that it was easily available to anyone who wanted to find out. After all, she took responsibility for organising the kitchen at the cricket club when a visiting team was playing, and it was on the club's website as their contact, as well as on the noticeboard in the clubhouse. It was on the list of people who could fix up collections of donations of big items at the charity shop, and all over the information relating to the various clubs and committees at the school or the golf club, which she had served on from time to time. She had kept the same number through several generations of mobile phones, and realised her contact details were all too visible.

She had thought to go to the police when it first started, of course. But that would mean it would all come out, and her well-ordered life would be ruined. Elliot would hate her and might take the kids away. She could not bear that, so she paid as instructed each month to buy the silence of whoever was doing this.

The only person she could tell was Guy, of course. And she didn't even tell *him* for the first couple of months. She was scared it would frighten him away.

Chapter 6

Emma had planned a new route for her morning run, and the horror of finding the body had started to recede.

At this time of year, with the morning sun low in the sky by the time she returned to her flat, she was often dazzled by the light pouring in through the kitchen window, opposite the front door, when she got back from her run. Whilst it meant she sometimes had to stand up to eat her breakfast, if the sun was too bright to sit at the table, it did improve her mood as she made ready to face the working day.

There seemed to be no progress on catching the killer, although it was now all over the papers and there were newspaper reporters outside the office in the street, or hanging about in the coffee shops in town.

Clearly the press loved an unsolved murder, and were striking fear into the hearts of would-be visitors to the town by publishing lurid suggestions that a killer still stalked the streets.

Elliots, following advice from the Local Council, had taken some precautions. Nobody was supposed to travel for work to view houses on their own, and there were warnings about being out alone after dark. Although she was not too concerned about it, Emma's morning run now took in the main road, and apart from a short section along the narrow cliff path, past the tall wall and the gate at the bottom of Elliot's garden, was principally around the well-lit roads on the housing estate where she lived.

The only time she went out apart from that, other than back and forth to work, was to attend her busy yoga class on Thursday evenings in the community hall.

Emma was not much of a believer in the spiritual benefits of yoga, but they were a nice crowd, and she got to chat with Peter, if he was there.

Peter was apparently a divorcee, and about her own age, or slightly older. He worked in a Government Office of some description, and so far, Emma had established that he lived alone in one of the popular and classy apartments one row back from the sea front, at the end of the town.

Emma rather hoped he would pluck up the courage to ask her out one day, but as the weeks of yoga classes rolled on, there was no progress on that front.

She had to be content to chat to him over a cup of the mostly tasteless herbal tea they dished out after the class, before everyone drifted off.

***

Karen's dad dropped her off at the cricket ground, and they set a time for him to return to pick her up.

She had allowed herself to be talked into helping with the cricket teas because Mikey was playing. It was only a second team match against an apparently lacklustre side from a nearby village, but Mikey had suggested she might pop along. And whilst it wasn't like a proper date, Karen thought it was a start, and agreed to lend a hand in the kitchen.

Mikey looked cool in his cricket whites and was obviously popular among the other players and the old boys who hung about watching the game, or visited the bar in the clubhouse. While the players were on the field, and she had nothing to do, she caught snatches of conversations going on around the boundary.

The main topic was the murder, of course. Jack, the opposing team's captain, said 'I heard he'd been stabbed with a massive zombie knife,' which made Karen shudder.

***

They found little of interest except a few unpaid bills and an old mobile phone in a drawer, which would be sent for analysis. That was until, as the search of the cottage continued, one of the technicians carefully placed a letter he found from the victim's son, Andrew, in a clear evidence bag.

The letter was one of several they had found, and DS Curtis read the handwritten note without much interest until he turned the bag over to read the second and final page.

"Dear Dad," the letter started. "I had 50g of Alpen with Greek-style yoghurt and a banana and 400ml of semi-skimmed milk for my breakfast today, same as always. I'm going to have 200g of beans on toast for my lunch with a 330ml can of Seven-Up. Guy has put the beans in a pot in the microwave, ready for me, and I can do the toast on my own (two slices of white).

"My therapy session at Dr Brown's went better yesterday because there was nobody in the waiting room, and I didn't see anyone in the park when I was walking over there, or on the way back. But when I got back and let myself into the flat, there were people there."

DS Curtis turned over.

"Guy had come back from the gallery, although he should have been at work, and Panda Markham was here, and they both had no clothes on.

"They hadn't seen me come in, so I went to get my sketch pad and then watched what they were doing for a while. Then the telephone rang, and Panda jumped up. When she saw me, she shouted at me and ran into the bathroom.

"Then they both shouted at me, so I went into the studio and stayed there, writing this letter and working on the sketches I had started, until they had gone.

"My sketches were not good, and I will need to try again after lunch today. I've never been able to capture how people move, as I have told you before, but it was useful to see them without clothes, which distorts the body shape. If I can do better sketches, which I like a bit more, I'll send some of them to you, so you can tell me if I have got it right.

"I tried to show the first one to Guy when he made me come out for dinner, but he told me to tear it up.

"You asked about my money when you wrote last time, and the time before. I've already told you several times that Guy manages all that, so please don't worry."

The letter was signed with a scrawl, and DS Curtis

sat down at the dining table to read it again. This was not like any of the other brief letters, notes really, that the team had found, and he wondered what it meant.

Chapter 7

The previous March, before the murder.

As February turned to March, Stan had to face it. The catch was getting poorer and poorer, and he was struggling to make a living. Perhaps it was just a bad spell. But if it was, it was the worst he could remember.

It was getting depressing, and sometimes he even considered selling up to the Richards. But he could not bring himself to do it, although he had to accept that he did need a way to supplement his income, if he was going to keep the boat.

He tried car boot sales, disposing of all the accumulated junk of a lifetime. He sold his van and bought an older, cheaper car. And he even sold one of Andrew's paintings to the owner of the auction house that Guy had originally worked for.

That had kept his head above water for a while, but he could not rid himself of the guilt he felt at selling the painting, especially without telling Andrew. It was only a small early one and lacked the skill and accomplishment of his later work, and Andrew had not thought enough of it to take it with him to London when he moved. But it still wasn't really Stan's to sell.

If only things had been simpler, or if they had produced another son who could have gone into the business when it was clear Andrew was not capable of helping him with the boat. But in his loveless marriage, that wasn't going to happen.

Now that she was no longer here, he regretted how badly he had treated Irene. All the fights and the shouting. It wasn't her fault, after all. After Andrew was born, there would be no more children. And it became clearer, as the boy grew, that all his hopes of passing the boat on were bound to remain unfulfilled.

They thought of nothing else but Andrew, and exhausted themselves in their efforts to understand and manage his problems. They went to doctors and all sorts of supposed experts, and spent fortunes on trying to find ways to help.

Irene read about his condition day and night, looking, if not for a cure, then for a way to cope.

But it was no good. The situation just got worse and worse. Until they discovered that the only way to keep him calm was to give him paper and pencils, and eventually canvas and an easel and let him draw and paint.

Irene started bringing home books about art, and he devoured them, staying up for days and nights reading. Then she got an iPad, and they started looking things up together. That was until he got so obsessed with it that she had to give it to him and let him learn on his own.

The school said he was really bright, but that they couldn't cope with him once he was a teenager, and they had to move him to a special school. Irene had to get a job to pay for that, and often worked double shifts to keep up with it.

At least that was where they came across Dr Brown, who was an accomplished expert with children like Andrew. And later, when he left the school to set up his own consultancy in London, he offered to continue working with Andrew. That helped a lot.

The fishing was good then, fortunately, or they would never have managed. But then Irene's friend from work suggested showing some of Andrew's pictures to an art expert, and after that, everything changed.

But he knew that what was nagging at him now was concern for what Andrew was doing, and if he was all right in London? Was he happy, or at least what passed for happy in his world?

He knew Guy regarded him as the protege he had discovered and was looking after him. But was that just to keep him painting and to make money out of him?

And why couldn't he get a straight answer about where Andrew's money went and what these 'investments' Guy was making for him were?

He was having to work seven days a week to make enough to put food on his own table and pay the bills, as things were, otherwise he would have gone up to London to see for himself the conditions Andrew was living in and find out what was going on. But he couldn't even afford the train ticket, let alone anything else.

So he had relied on the letters.

Andrew depended on a rigid routine, so when it became part of his ritual to send a regular letter home, Stan asked for information in his replies. But because the boy didn't understand anything but the most direct way of asking questions, he was not getting satisfactory responses.

As a result, he worried more and more and tried to ask the same questions in different ways to get to the bottom of what was happening, so far away in London.

Stan suspected Guy read the letters and may have

got the impression that he wanted money from Andrew. While he was undoubtedly coming up short at the moment, that was not the point. He could look after himself. What he wanted to know was if Andrew was being exploited, and his suspicions were growing.

Andrew's last letter gave him what could amount to proof.

The letter revealed that the woman called Panda or, he thought, Amanda was her actual name, was in on it. Her father, he knew, was Sir Lemuel, his landlord, who owned his cottage. Rumour had it that she was spoilt, had expensive tastes, and only the best of everything was good enough for her. A typical product of the overprivileged upper classes, he thought. And now Andrew had seen her cheating on her husband, and having it off with Guy!

Were they living off Andrew's earnings? Why should *she* have access to Andrew's money? Hadn't she got enough of her own?

If she was playing away and getting money from Guy, he thought, and if that money was Andrew's, perhaps her husband, or even her father, might like to know about it.

***

Now that the weather was improving, Emma

stepped up her efforts on her morning run.

Having recently signed up for a yoga class as well, she should soon be feeling much fitter, and hopefully would lose a bit of weight too.

She liked to run along the beach, from the little jetty where the fishing boats moored, in front of the cottages, down past the cafe, round the headland and on past the beach huts. Then she would go up the steep cliff path, along past the end of Elliot and Panda's garden, and out onto the road at the junction by the pub. After that, she would either go down the lane and into the housing estate, or along past the church and the shops, and double back beside the holiday caravans, through the wood by the golf course, and home.

She found the last winter had dragged, and she had lost motivation, so now that the spring was here at last, she propelled herself on, determined to blow away the cobwebs.

She had to keep sharp, now that she was left in charge of the office so much. The trust Elliot had in her was growing with each new set of sales figures, and she knew that the manager's job he had dangled was hers for the taking if she kept it up.

Not that there had been much to be a manager of previously. But now that Karen, the school leaver, had joined the firm, things were slowly changing.

While Elliot was careful about expanding too rapidly and cautious in his plans, she did know that he hoped to open another branch in the not-too-distant future, and when that happened, she wanted to be ready.

Chapter 8

On the day of the murder.

It was another rainy September morning, and Panda hated rain.

Now that the school holidays were over, things had returned to some sort of routine. So early in the morning, between showers, when Elliot left to take the boys to school in the Range Rover, Panda drove the short distance to her father's farmhouse in her VW Golf.

She was excited about the visit she had arranged at her father's house, due in a couple of hours or so. At last, she had convinced her father to finally get a couple of the old paintings in his house valued. These particular pictures had looked down at her as she grew up, and she had never liked the forbidding faces they featured, which seemed to be accusing her of being up to no good. It had taken her a while to convince him to do it, but today Guy was due to come and evaluate the paintings on behalf of his gallery, possibly with a view to their sale.

She was there before the meeting because she also had to collect two new bicycles, delivered to the farm, so the boys did not see them before their birthday.

She met the postman on the drive to the farmhouse as she pulled up.

This same postman had been delivering here for many years, and they exchanged greetings. Panda commented that he was delivering early today. Smiling, he explained that he wanted to finish and get home because his grandson was expected for tea, and he gave Panda the post to take in.

Farmers start work early, and the distinctive upright profile of Sir Lemuel Fulton-Marks could just be made out through the raindrops on the window, with his back to the house, on the long lawn some distance away. He was discussing something with her brother, who nowadays was responsible for the day-to-day running of the family farm. They were standing under a broad golf umbrella and were too far away to call, so Panda dropped the post on the big old refectory table in the main hallway.

As the letters slid over one another, she noticed that one of them was in one of the estate agent's distinctive envelopes with its gummed flap on the short side, rather than at what might usually be regarded as the top, on the long side. The envelope had obviously been reused, with a piece of thick white paper sellotaped down and covering up the original address label, and a new stamp placed over the old one. It had a handwritten address to Sir Lemuel. She picked it up and almost had a panic attack …it must be him … the blackmailer, now writing to her father!

Without hesitation, she ripped off the copiously applied sticky tape used to re-seal the envelope and pulled out the note within, which was written on thick white paper.

The letter was set out in peculiar, slightly unnatural, short staccato sentences, and in tightly spaced capital letters, but it was all in there. Everything he had threatened her with exposing and more. The details of her affair with Guy, who the author wrote lived with Andrew Gurney somewhere in London, and was using him to make money; and now the accusation that Panda and Guy were not just lovers but were working together to defraud Andrew of the proceeds of his work.

Predictably, the letter was unsigned.

She read the note twice and decided it was time she finished this, once and for all.

Glancing up, she saw her father was still deep in conversation down at the far end of the garden. She decided that he could not have seen her and was therefore not aware that she had arrived.

Then she looked thoughtfully at the big fireplace set just to her right, with the old-fashioned telephone and the telephone card index beside it. She saw the tall display case to one side, which housed her great-grandfather's collection of dusty old African memorabilia, and an idea crystallised in her mind.

Standing on tiptoes, he opened the topmost door of the tall cabinet above her head and felt around until her fingers found what she was looking for. She knew there was a Zulu "iklwa" in there, behind a dusty ox-hide shield.

She remembered the stories her grandfather told to frighten her and her brother when they were small, involving this spear and others like it in the small collection. In her mind, she could hear him describing in detail how the Zulu warriors would use the efficient long, flat-bladed "iklwa", designed for close combat stabbing.

Her grandfather impressed on the children that they must never play with these artefacts, and stored them well out of their reach. However, he delighted in telling them that the name "iklwa" is said to derive from the distinctive sound it made when the short spear was withdrawn from a victim's body. She had never forgotten that grim description of its lethal efficiency.

She reached in and took the still sharp weapon carefully from the cabinet, and ran her hands over the length of it. A small piece of the leather binding fell off as she examined it. She picked it up and held it against the letter. Then, opening the telephone card index, she ran her fingernail down the list and searched for a name. When she found it, she picked up the telephone handset and dialled the number, pushing the letter with its sticky tape into the back pocket of her jeans as she waited for the call to be answered.

When Stanley Gurney picked up, and giving him no opportunity to speak, she rapidly stated that his son, Andrew, was in trouble and she urgently needed to talk to him about his welfare.

'I'll meet you at the beach huts in ten minutes, you will find the door of one of them unlocked. Go in and wait for me there.'

Before he could start to ask questions, Panda ended the call.

Glancing down the garden, she saw that her father was still deep in conversation with her brother, some distance away. She was confident that they could not have seen her.

Then she picked up the ancient spear and ran to her car.

Turning round in the wide driveway, she drove down towards the sea front and the makeshift shingle car parking area behind the beach huts.

***

Yesterday, and the day before, after work, she and Karen had spent time cleaning up the beach huts. It was a task the Elliots' staff always performed at the end of each summer season.

This time, Elliot had given the boys their tea so that Panda could do the job.

Karen went straight home when they finished each day, and Panda had put all the keys of the little wooden buildings in the glove compartment of her car, ready to take them back to the office when it reopened this morning.

Now she opened the glove compartment and grabbed the first key that came to hand, and noticed that the tag attached to it had the name 'Manilla' written next to the identification number.

Panda remembered the hut in question had a bright green door that stuck in the frame and was difficult to open. When she visited before to clean it, she also noticed that it seemed unused, and although dusty, it did not need very much cleaning. It would do nicely.

Now that she had seen the re-used envelope, which, of course, she recognised was one of those she had used to send the blackmailer money, Panda was convinced that she knew precisely who was behind all the threats and intimidation she had endured for so long.

To compound her theory, when she stopped at the little shingle car park, she drew the envelope out of her pocket and peeled off some of the paper sellotaped over the original label. There she found the address of the PO Box she had used in the past to send the blackmailer money, in her own handwriting.

She thought the unusual sentence structure in the letter might have been used as an attempt to disguise the sender's identity, but who, other than Andrew's father, would know about Guy and Andrew? And only the blackmailer would have had access to that particular envelope.

She grabbed the short Zulu spear from the seat beside her and thrust the letter into the back pocket of her jeans as she climbed out of the car and ran down the slope towards the sea.

Panda let herself into the beach hut, pushing the sticking door wide open. Then she set the latch, pushed the door almost shut, and waited inside.

The door had swollen. It stuck in its frame slightly and did not close completely, but now she stood behind the door, in the tight space on the hinge side, so that when Stan arrived, she would not be seen until she shut the door. She had chosen to set the door on the latch so that Stan could enter, and she could do what she had decided to do.

She said nothing when he came through the door, and her attack needed just two quick upward thrusts of the blade, with the palm of her hand on the rounded end of the handle, and pushing it with all her strength up under his ribcage.

Stan registered shock when she stepped out from behind the door and attacked him, but had no time to make any sound.

The first thrust made him topple backwards, and she used the force of his retreat to pull the short spear out of his abdomen against the suction. The second thrust was delivered as he lurched towards her, trying to grab her, but he collapsed onto the floor, and, gasping, rolled onto his back.

She struggled to do it, but she pulled the blade out again.

There was the confirmation of the horrible noise from the stories her grandfather scared her with, and which the blade is said to be named after. When the suction was released, she heard it. "Iklwa".

Whilst she had to pull hard to get the implement out of his body, she could see at a glance that he was dead.

Pausing only to catch her breath and throw an old rug over the body, she kicked open the door and rushed down to the water. There she washed off the traces of blood on the blade in the sea. She noticed with satisfaction that the receding tide broke up the small amount of blood and washed it rapidly away.

When it was done, in her anxiousness to leave, she forgot that she had left the sticking door on the latch, and having paused only to pull it too, she ran for her car.

She drove to her father's house once again and arrived with an hour to spare before Guy's arrival was planned. Walking in unannounced through the open front door, and before anyone saw her, she replaced the weapon in the cabinet exactly where she found it.

'Can't stop, Pop,' she said as her father appeared from the kitchen, seconds later. 'I just need to pick up the boys' new bikes, ready for their birthday and nip into the office for something. I'll be back in time for the meeting.'

The seasons she spent learning to act in the local

amateur dramatic society some years ago, before the boys were born, helped her to keep her voice steady and her expression neutral, although, inside, she could feel a rising tide of panic building as she contemplated what she had just done. Her father must never know, of course, so, as she had learned back then, she carefully got into character and kept her voice calm.

'Right-ho,' said her father. 'I hid them in the tool store by the garages when you had them delivered here. I guessed the boys were unlikely to look in there, if they were up here. Are you going to wrap them up?'

'I'll try, but bikes are such difficult things to wrap.'

'Crepe paper,'

'Pardon?'

'Crepe paper, my dear. Well, it will still look like a bike, of course, but at least it will look a bit festive. That is what we used to wrap your first proper bike, and you seemed pleased enough.'

'Oh, it was lovely, Pop. I adored it, and I remember that Christmas as one of the best.'

'Well, it is the twins' birthday rather than Christmas, of course, but the principle is the same.'

Panda nodded and turned to walk over to the tool

store.

'Panda? Is that blood on your T-shirt?'

Mortified, Panda looked where he was pointing. She was sure she had been so careful, but there were two small bloody finger marks on her left side, by her hip. Her mind was on fire. How had this happened? How had she missed this?

'Panda?'

'Oh, it's just a paper cut, Pop.' She surprised herself with the speed and plausibility of her response. 'Elliots cheapo envelopes often get me like that, when I'm doing the mail-out,' she managed.

'Oh? Well, make sure you are back when this fellow arrives. What's his name again?'

'Guy Lombardi,' she said. 'Now I must dash, I have got so much to do!'

With the children's bikes safely in the hatchback and her heart pumping, Panda tried to calm down as she climbed into the car and told herself to breathe.

Anxious to get there before any of the staff turned up for work, she drove straight to the estate agent's office and used her key. There, she returned all the beach hut keys to their security box on the wall, and she was back in the car five minutes before Emma was due to arrive to open for business.

Then she drove rapidly home to wash the blood out of her T-shirt. She still had a mountain of things to do, but it was over now, and she must make herself relax and act naturally.

She had to be ready in fresh clothes and looking her best for Guy.

When the business with her father was concluded, and they were on their own, she longed to hold him in her arms. His soothing presence would help her to deal with what she had done.

While obviously she could never tell him about it, she did plan to tell him about the letter, at least. She was certain that the result of her actions would enable them to continue their tryst. They could remain lovers now, without the danger of a blackmailer preying on her mind.

***

After concealing the new bikes by pushing them into the clutter in the old lawnmower shed, halfway down the garden, she took her jeans and her tee shirt out of the washing machine and threw them into the tumble dryer. The cup of coffee she had made before she went in the shower was almost cold, but she drank it anyway as she re-read the letter more carefully and focused particularly on the accusation that she and Guy were defrauding Andrew.

Unlikely though that was, she thought, it gave the blackmailer a premise on which to base his twisted threats, this time sent to her father.

She smiled to think that there would be no more of that now, and she was grateful she had caught the letter before her father saw it. But although the suggestion that Guy might not be honest did briefly surprise her, she dismissed the notion almost immediately.

Guy was wonderful. Everything to her. All that Elliot wasn't, although he did his best. The thought that her lover might not be all he seemed was incredible, unworthy even. She put the idea out of her mind as she dressed in fresh clothes, smart but nothing too dressy, added a little light make-up, and prepared to introduce her lover to her father, and to the paintings at her former home.

It was the following morning that Emma found the body.

Chapter 9

One week later

Now that the horror of finding the body had begun to recede, and life had returned to something resembling normal, Emma had decided to make a special effort this week.

Peter, at the yoga class, had long enough to pluck up courage to ask her out, and hadn't made a move, although all the signs were there that he wanted to. So now it was time to push matters along and grasp the initiative herself.

Generally speaking, she wore only minimal make-up, but this afternoon, when she returned from work, she spent some time in front of the mirror and did the best she could to disguise nature's ravages and show herself in her best light.

The day before, she had managed to get an evening appointment, had her hair done, and she had freshly painted her nails.

But for the ultimate touch, she had ordered a new

one-piece body suit, which was much tighter and cut differently than her trusty old leggings and tank top. She had noticed the leader of the group wearing a similar one and asked her where she got it. Now she had it on, it emphasised her curves a lot less subtly, and as she smoothed it down in front of the mirror, she thought it looked quite sexy, without actually being tarty. This, she thought, was the height of 'yoga class fashion'.

Whereas the group leader wore black, Emma opted for a shimmering dark pink, or was it even a shade of purple, for her clingy new outfit. She almost changed her mind about the revealing garment, but decided that if she was ever going to provoke a response from Peter, it was now or never.

And it worked.

As she tried to swallow some of the bland herbal tea without wincing as the class broke up, Peter asked her out for a drink.

***

This time it was just 'practice nets', she had been told. But Mikey said they usually had a drink after the session in the clubhouse, and invited Karen along.

Once again, her father dropped her off at the cricket ground, but this time, as her 'date' clashed with a long-standing invitation to supper for her parents at her grandmother's, it was agreed that Mikey would drop Karen and some of the other team members home.

Mikey explained that it was his turn to drive a couple of the players home, because they took it in turns to be the 'designated driver'. That meant he could not have an alcoholic drink, and she would not be alone in the car.

Karen was wearing her new trainers and her tightest jeans when she arrived at the cricket club.

***

Elliot noticed Panda seemed uptight and asked if she was OK.

Panda had bought a new yellow dress with a narrow waist. It was a bit shorter than she would usually wear, but she decided it showed off her long legs, and she wanted to dazzle Guy when she saw him again. She paired it with high-heeled sandals and a colour-coordinated clutch bag.

Obviously, she was not going out dressed like that, and her outfit was carefully folded in her overnight bag, which was waiting in the hall.

'I'm fine,' replied Panda. 'Just a bit concerned. Sophie said her mother had taken a turn for the worse and sounded really worried.'

'Well, did you want me to drive you up there instead of going on the train? It might be quicker.'

'No, it's OK, sweetheart. I've been to Sophie's house several times before, as you know, and it is just a short cab ride from the mainline station, so I'll be fine.'

'Well, if you are sure …'

'No problem. My taxi to the station at this end is booked anyway and should be here in about ten minutes. Now will you be all right putting the boys to bed?'

'Of course, don't worry. We will be fine.'

When the taxi arrived, Elliot gave her a peck on the cheek and carried her bag out to the car.

'Be good, honey, and I'll see you tomorrow,' he said.

Wrapping her thin summer coat around her, Panda climbed into the taxi and smiled at him as they drove away. She had absolutely no intention of being good at all.

**

In his consulting rooms, Dr Tomas Brown sat down behind his desk with a sigh.

As a behavioural psychologist and neurologist,

specialising in Autism and ADHT he thought he had seen it all, but Andrew Gurney continued to surprise him.

When the boy moved to his current address, on the other side of the park from the consulting rooms, Dr Brown thoroughly supported the idea and even became involved in helping to find a suitable apartment, enabling Andrew to keep up his twice-weekly visits with the minimum of stress.

The boy was undoubtedly a genius, at least as far as his ability to paint and draw was concerned, but the more usual social skills we take for granted had to be learnt, and re-learnt, and Dr Brown had an uphill and a seemingly never-ending struggle with that. Now, as he approached his twenties, Andrew was still likely to fall back into his old withdrawn ways.

Since he was thirteen, when they first met, he had witnessed tantrums, morose moods, and the full range of awkward behaviours, although now he was much calmer. That calmness was fragile and came at a price, however. Guy, his protector and sometime representative, had his work cut out to keep Andrew on track, and had to manage everything from ensuring he was eating to making sure he had enough paints, canvases and sketch-pads to continue to produce his remarkable art.

Progress had been made with Andrew's self-imposed isolation however; he could be trusted to walk along the pavement by the park and back to the consulting rooms on his own. Although, as far as Dr Brown knew, that was the limit of his ventures into the outside world, and he was still very easily distracted.

Last week, for example, Andrew was slightly late for his session. That was so unlike him that Dr Brown looked out of his window over the park to see if he could see him coming. After the death of his father, he was concerned that the boy might become withdrawn again and might stop attending their sessions.

There was Andrew, apparently staring at the post box on the corner of the road, with his hands in his coat pockets, and just as Dr Brown resolved to go down to see if he was all right, he seemed to shake himself and then continued on his short journey. No amount of questioning could elicit what he thought he was doing, and apart from apologising for being late, he would say nothing about why he was just standing, staring.

Dr Brown opened the file and updated his notes, and hoped that their next session would be more straightforward.

Chapter 10

Mikey was all hands, and she had to push him off twice.

To start with, after they had dropped off the last of the cricket players at his home, she didn't mind at all and enjoyed the kissing. She didn't even object when Mikey quite skilfully undid her bra. But after a bit more of that, she realised it had to stop, so she broke away from him and told him that was enough.

To be fair, he accepted what she said and allowed her to readjust her clothing before driving her to her front door, where he said he hoped he hadn't upset her and asked if he could see her again.

'I'm not, like, saying I don't want to see you. I do. But I'm only just seventeen, Mikey, and I want to wait a bit yet,' she said. 'How about you take me to the pictures or something like that? A proper date, like.'

'Sure,' he had replied. 'No problem. I'll call you.'

Karen was in tears when she reached her bedroom. In all the cheap novels she had read, when the guy said "I'll call you," it meant that was the last the heroine would see of him.

***

As she prepared to walk from the carpark to the pub, Emma told herself again that she must not appear desperate.

She was forty now, she reminded herself, and had quite a bit of experience with men. This was nothing new.

But it was all such a long time ago. It had been almost five years since she left King and Rutter, said goodbye to Simon Hamilton-Smythe, and moved to the coast. They had lived together for eighteen months, until Emma realised that she was just there to wash his squash kit and cook his meals.

Working for King and Rutter had been good for her career, though, and she had learned all the 'ins and outs' of being a 'negotiator' in an estate agency there. To some extent, she had Simon to thank for that, as they worked in the same office, and he gave her plenty of guidance.

In their spare time, she also got into running with Simon, and their lives seemed quite settled. But there came a point when it was obvious she was going no further in her career, or her relationship.

Before that, there was Steve, of course. Her first

serious boyfriend. She found herself washing his football kit and his gym gear. Although on that occasion he had left her and had broken her heart.

Since then, anything resembling romance had eluded her, and for a while, wrapped up in the job and trying to make herself indispensable at Elliots, she all but gave up.

Peter at the yoga class reignited a spark, however, and now she had a date.

She checked her appearance one last time in the sun-blind mirror and sighed. It would have to do.

'Here goes nothing,' she muttered under her breath as she opened the car door.

***

On this occasion, Guy and Panda had their clothes back on and were making coffee in the kitchen when Andrew returned after his therapy session with Dr Brown.

Panda knew there was something wrong.

Guy had seemed remote somehow. They had gone through the motions, but it must be said, not with the usual passion and urgency, on his part at least. Nothing had been said, but when it was over, Panda knew something had changed.

Before she travelled to London, Panda had re-read the intercepted letter the blackmailer had sent to her father. The accusation that she and Guy were defrauding Andrew was nonsense, of course, but it had bothered her, and she thought she should discuss it with Guy. She prepared herself to tell him about it now.

'Guy,' she asked, 'Andrew must have made a lot of money from his paintings? What does he do with his money?'

Guy made a dismissive gesture as they became aware of Andrew turning his key in the lock and letting himself in, just as Panda was ready to get the letter from her handbag in the bedroom and show it to him.

For a moment, Guy was distracted as he made sure Andrew was all right and got him water, before he scuttled into his studio and closed the door, without really acknowledging Panda.

When she tried to ask again, gently holding his arm, Guy became defensive and told her to mind her own business in a low, angry voice she had never heard before.

'Actually, Panda, that is private business. None of it has anything to do with you, and you are so clingy,' he said, shaking off her hand. 'I need a bit of space, and I think it might be better …'

'Guy?'

'Look, there is no easy way to say this. We are finished, Panda, and I don't want you to come here again.'

Panda dropped the full coffee cup she was holding onto the sink and recoiled in shock.

The noise brought Andrew out of his studio.

'Actually,' he said, 'I would like to know how much money I have, and where it is, too.'

Guy looked as though he was going to explode, and snarled through gritted teeth. And she hadn't even been able to show him the letter yet.

'Panda was just leaving, and I will explain it all to you, Andrew, as soon as she has gone,' he said. 'Go and get your things, Panda.'

Panda felt hot tears in her eyes, and although Andrew was watching, the shock of it made her unable to contain herself.

'Please, Guy. Oh, please! I'll do anything. Anything you want, just please don't send me away. I love you!'

Guy grabbed her arm roughly and propelled her into

the bedroom. Now clearly in a dangerous rage, he picked up her bag and began stuffing the rest of her clothes, and even the towel she had used after her shower, back into it.

'Get out, Panda,' he shouted. 'I never want to see you again.'

'No! Please. Oh, stop, Guy. Can't we talk about this? Please ... please!'

Thrusting her bag into her arms, Guy hustled Panda out of the front door and down the first couple of concrete stairs.

Then he let go of her arm and, without its support, she stumbled.

As Guy turned back into the flat and slammed the door, she tripped and collided with the bare brick wall, cutting her elbow. Before she knew what was happening, she lost her footing and fell forward, missing the last few steps and landing heavily on her knees on the pavement.

Unable to see through her tears, she knelt there for a moment, surrounded by the contents of her bag, as she tried to catch her breath.

She became aware of the presence of an old woman beside her.

'Took a bit of a tumble, dearie? Here, let me help you

up.'

Shuddering with shock and grief, Panda allowed the woman to take her arm.

'Had a bit to drink, have we? Not to worry, we will soon have you as right as rain. Alright if I use this towel to wipe up this drop of blood on your knees?'

***

A few moments earlier, three members of the Richards family were walking towards the bend in the road by the park, a short distance over the road from the archway, which gave onto the stone steps leading to Guy and Andrew's flat. They were led by Betty, who clutched some legal papers in her pudgy hand.

'Leave the talking to me, you two,' she said, not for the first time.

'Er, mum,' said Errol, looking behind them down the road.

'What Errol? What is it now?'

'There is a police car, and I think that is the bloke who came to our house what's getting out.'

Betty swivelled round and saw DS Curtis and a WPC approaching with another uniformed officer.

'Bollocks,' said Betty. 'Keep walking straight on, boys. And don't look back. We won't be able to pay a call here today, I'm afraid.'

***

'Wasn't that …'

'Yes, I believe it was, Linda. It seems the Richards have found out where Andrew Gurney lives. That might change things in terms of keeping him safe.'

'Do you think they would hurt Andrew, sir?'

'Not physically, perhaps, but they might try to intimidate him, which, given how they look, would not take much.'

'These fishing licences must be pretty valuable if they are prepared to travel to London mob-handed to try to get one.'

'Crabbing permits, Linda. And they are not issuing any more since global warming, so they are like gold dust.'

'But I thought anyone could go crabbing. On the pier you see kids …'

'It's not so much the crabs, although they do have a value, Linda. It's the lobsters that they catch out at sea as well. That's where the money is.'

As they rounded the bend, the Richards disappeared from view in the labyrinth of roads ahead, and the archway by the door came into view. The sight that greeted them caused them to break into a run.

Slumped on the pavement, a woman was being assisted by an older woman who was mopping up what appeared to be blood.

***

Running up, the policewoman saw the blood and asked if there had been a road traffic accident. She got no reply.

'I think she is a tom and her bloke just chucked her down those stairs,' said the old lady. 'First off, I thought she was pissed, but she don't smell of it.'

DS Curtis, realising that violence had been involved, and the younger woman was the victim of an attack, suggested abruptly that either she should pull herself together and tell them what has happened, or she should prepare to explain it all down at the station.

Linda, the WPC, was crouching by the weeping Panda.

'What's your name, love?' she asked, but Panda just shook her head and buried her face in her bloodied hands.

'Pretty for a hooker,' observed the other male uniformed police officer to his colleagues. 'But maybe they can afford a better class of scrubber round here.'

'Wait a minute,' said DS Curtis, looking more closely. 'Don't I know you? ... Yes, hang on ... aren't you Elliot's wife ...'

The WPC and the local police officer looked at him in confusion.

'From the cricket club ... yes. I'm sure of it now. Teddy, no, Panda, isn't it?'

****

The archway, which led to a small cobbled courtyard and the eight or nine stone steps up to the door of Guy and Andrew's flat, sat between two upmarket shops.

With a wide frontage facing the road, the premises of a bespoke shirt-maker was set under the flat itself, and the narrow shop front of a jeweller's shop stood on the other side of the stone arch, a little higher up the hill. The road and the contour of the land sloped so that the steps to the flat were higher than their counterpart on the opposite side. The little cobbled courtyard itself was divided by wide steps to create two small level areas, rising up the slope.

The small courtyard had a secondary door to the side of the shirt-maker's store, under the stone steps, but was otherwise just used as space to store the bins these days.

Panda had fallen down the last of the steps and over the cobbled area and ended up on the other side of the arch, on the pavement, beside the road.

When DS Curtis remembered her name, Panda was shocked out of her grief and looked up at him.

'It is Panda, isn't it?' he asked. 'How did this happen, and what are you doing here?'

'I just …'

'She ain't pissed, I don't think,' said the older woman, gathering herself and getting to her feet as the WPC took over. 'Drugs more n'like. You gonna call an ambulance?'

DS Curtis looked at his colleague from the local force, who confirmed that he was already making the call.

'I was … I came from the flat up there, and tripped on the stairs when he … when he …'

'When he what?' Now on her feet with her hands on her hips, the bystander still had plenty to say. 'Looks like your boyfriend threw you out, ta me.'

'I'm sorry, who exactly are you?' said DS Curtis, and then, looking at the other constable, 'We shall need a statement.'

Panda was struggling to her feet and trying to gather up the contents of her bag.

'While you do that,' he said, 'I think we should see what the people in that flat up there have to say for themselves. Can you walk, young lady?'

***

Panda wanted to run away.

The last thing she wanted to do was face Guy again. But the police seemed to want to keep them all together, and walked the little party up the steps.

Now at the top, they arrived at the door to the apartment, and DS Curtis knocked sharply.

'Now we will find out what has been going on,' he said, with more confidence than he felt.

Guy looked through the peephole, and seeing Panda, who he assumed was alone, he shouted through the door.

'I told you we were through! Now fuck off, Panda,

before I call the police.'

The DS Curtis cleared his throat, knocked on the door once more, identified himself as a police officer, and insisted that Guy must open the door.

'The police are already here, as it happens, sir. Now will you please open the door.'

Andrew tried to disappear into the squashy upholstery of the tatty sofa, and with his feet tucked up under him, clutched one of the large cushions to his chest.

***

As Panda was hustled up the steps, the letter fell out of her bag.

WPC Linda picked it up and held onto it until they got into the flat. Once in, she put it on the kitchen table along with the rest of Panda's stuff.

As Panda started to gather the contents of her bag and picked up the letter, she let out a sob.

'If only you had let me show you this, Guy, you would have understood what I went through for you.'

'What is it?' asked Guy.

'It's another one of those letters. From him.'

DS Curtis asked to see the letter, and reluctantly Panda handed it over. He studied the torn envelope with its address labels and sellotape, before he drew out the letter and read it.

'And you say you don't know who sent this?'

'No,' said Guy. 'It's just malicious nonsense. Panda has had several like that. Is it another demand for money?'

'No. It is not asking for money or anything like that. But it seems to have been sent to alert the recipient,' DS Curtis nodded at Panda, 'your father, to your affair, and flag up your potential involvement in defrauding Andrew Gurney out of his money. Are there other lovers who might be jealous?'

'No, of course not. Guy and I ... I have never had a relationship like this before ...'

'Just the one infidelity then. Perhaps with a bit of fraud on the side.'

'It was nothing like that. Nothing!' Panda began to cry again and took another tissue from the box on the kitchen table.

'So who do you think sent this, then?'

'I did,' said Andrew.

***

Chapter 11

The paramedic finished cleaning up Panda's cuts and abrasions and packed away his equipment.

Mary, the little old lady who had helped Panda, had given a statement and been shown out. As the crowd in the flat began to reduce in size, Andrew emerged from the comforting folds of the sofa a little more.

'So why did you send this letter, Andrew?' asked WPC Linda, taking a seat near, but not too close to him.

'Because it is the truth, and I didn't know her husband's address,' he stated.

'But you did know the address of Sir Lemuel Fulton-Marks?'

'Yes. He owns my father's cottage, where I used to live.'

'*He* must be the blackmailer,' said Guy.

'Ask him where he got the envelope,' said Panda.

'Thank you, but I think it would be better if we were to ask the questions,' said DS Curtis. 'But now you come to mention it, Andrew, where did you get this envelope?'

'Is this really relevant?' said Guy. 'Surely this can all wait.'

'I found it in the kitchen bin, there, under the worktop. I already had a stamp,' said Andrew.

DS Curtis turned to Panda.

'And you recognise it?'

'Yes, that is my writing on the envelope, under the paper stuck over it. It must be one of the ones I used to send money in, to the blackmailer.'

'Nonsense,' said Guy, his anger beginning to show in his voice again. 'Andrew might have picked that up anywhere. His condition means ...'

'Thank you, sir,' DS Curtis interrupted. 'How much money did you send this person, Panda ... I mean Mrs Markham?'

'About six thousand pounds, over several months. Each time he demanded more.'

'And do you have any idea who might have been blackmailing you?'

'I thought I had an idea, but no. I was wrong,' Panda reached for another tissue as she realised that Andrew's father was not the blackmailer.

'It must have been Andrew,' said Guy.

'What makes you say that, sir?'

'Because of the envelope,' Panda looked from face to face. 'If Andrew found that here, then ... then ...'

'Then Andrew *was* the blackmailer,' said Guy. 'It is obvious.'

'No, it isn't,' said Andrew, emerging a little further from his cocoon. 'I sent the letter to Mrs Markham's father, but I didn't blackmail her. I thought he needed to know what she was doing, and I hoped he might help me to find out what Guy has done with my money.'

'What nonsense!' Guy's voice was raised now, and he was standing, clenching and unclenching his fists. 'Andrew obviously sent you those texts demanding money, and when you ran out of money and couldn't pay any more, he carried out his threat and wrote to your father!'

'I don't have a mobile phone,' said Andrew.

'Did the demands for money arrive by text?' asked DS Curtis.

'Yes,' said Panda, trying and failing to catch Guy's eye.

'How did you know Mrs Markham had run out of money, sir? I don't think anyone here mentioned that,' said DS Curtis, rising to his feet.

'I ... she ...' The colour had drained from Guy's face.

'When I sent the last payment,' supplied Panda, 'I put a note in with it to say that was the last time, as he had taken all the money I had easy access to without alerting my husband.'

'Who would have seen that note, Mrs Markham, do you think?'

WPC Linda moved to stand by the kitchen table.

'Well only me ... and the blackmailer ...'

Realisation slammed into Panda like an express train.

'Guy! Oh, Guy, how could you!' she wailed. 'You did it! It was you all the time ... You bastard! And you even tried to blame poor little Andrew!'

WPC Linda gently took her arm and started to lead her towards the door.

'And what the hell have you done with Andrew's money?' she called out as the WPC ushered her through the door.

'Yes,' echoed Andrew. 'What have you done with my money, Guy?'

Chapter 12

Detective Inspector Paul Francis followed Elliot into the back office of the estate agency and closed the door.

'Is this about the murder?' asked Elliot, pulling up a client chair.

'No, I'm afraid this is about something else, sir. I need to talk to you about your wife …'

'Oh God. Panda! Has she been hurt?'

***

This second date was a bit more like it, Emma thought.

Peter had been charming when they went for that drink, but now here they were in the expensive Thai restaurant at the end of the parade of shops.

Emma settled down into her comfortable velour-covered chair, where patrons were offered drinks before being shown through to the dining room, and prepared herself for the treat to come.

***

You could say this did count as a proper date, she supposed.

A bag of chips sitting on the wall at the top of the cliff was all right, and Mikey said they could go for a drink afterwards and play darts at the Nelson, over the road.

It was a pleasant enough evening, although it had rained earlier, and now that the trippers had gone home, they could enjoy the views across the beach as the sun began to set.

'Lovely, innit,' said Mikey, indicating the sunset. 'Romantic, like.'

'It's very pretty', replied Karen.

'So are you, babe.'

'Shut up!' Karen blushed.

Mikey smiled.

'Chips all right?'

'Mmm.'

***

Dr Brown was surprised and somewhat flustered by the call, but he accepted what he had to do and declared himself prepared to help.

Without Guy to look after him, Andrew would be completely adrift since … since his father was no longer around. And Andrew had nowhere else to turn.

He could not cope on his own, and until Dr Brown could organise professional carers and get Andrew to accept them, he would have to look after him himself.

Andrew, at least, seemed happy to accept the situation. That was something.

With Czechoslovakian ancestry, following his grandparents' escape from Nazi occupation, the Brown family had originally been known by the name 'Svoboda', which the young Tomas Brown was told meant 'free man'. But apart from the rare evenings when some of his relatives would come to his parents' home and sing the old songs, accompanied on a battered violin played by his great uncle Bohdan, nothing much was ever said about their heritage, at least in the modern Brown household.

When he finished university, the young Tomas did take a trip to Prague to take in some of the sights his grandparents had mentioned, but the past held little interest for him. The fascinating world of medicine and, particularly, psychiatric studies, however, filled his head almost to the exclusion of everything else.

There had been a girl once. A woman, really. Several years his senior. But it couldn't last, and she eventually went back to her husband. Since then, his promising career filled his every waking moment, and he thrived on it.

Along the way, with the publication of a successful academic book and various papers, alongside his work as a Consultant, he had gradually become quite comfortably off. Now, though, his careful approach to money was going to be tested a little, as somebody would have to pay for Andrew's care. He expected it to last at least until the police could unravel the complex tangle of companies and bank accounts where Guy said he had invested all Andrew's money.

But the boy was a special study for him, and with his profile, which even included a very brief television appearance of his work on the local news, after Andrew's first paintings were sold, his talents had captured the public's interest. Capitalising on that, Dr Brown reasoned, his personal ongoing involvement in his care may lead to another academic paper, which might be lucrative enough to cover the expenditure.

Looking at it another way, and judging from the prices achieved for Andrew's work when some of it had been sold in the past, Andrew's income could amount to quite a sum, and although Dr. Brown's consultancy fees would have undoubtedly have made a dent in the remaining funds over the years, there should still be plenty left to cover any costs.

At least Dr Brown hoped so. But until the full facts around what Guy had been doing with the money emerged, he would have to be prepared to step up to fill the void.

Dr Brown reached for the telephone on his desk again. Now he needed to get Andrew a lawyer.

Chapter 13

Andrew assumed that the knock on the door was Dr Brown arriving to look after him as arranged, and he went to answer it.

As he opened the door, he was immediately blinded by a flash of light.

'Andrew Gurney?' said a voice. 'Could we just have a few words for the Daily News? Mind if we come in?'

With the effects of the flash still blinding him, Andrew tried to push the door shut, but of course, the leader of the team of journalists, now on the doorstep, had firmly planted his foot in the way.

'Who are you? What do you want?' managed Andrew.

'Mike Gillespie, Daily News. What was your reaction to learning about your father's murder? Were you still in touch with him? Had you had a row?'

'Go away!' said Andrew, trying again to force the

door closed.

'Have you sold any more paintings lately? Did you make much? Was your father looking after your money?'

'Leave me alone!'

'Fallen out with your father, have you? Who do you think murdered him?'

Although the effects of the flash were still affecting Andrew, he became aware that there were three people standing outside the door, but that somebody was bustling up the steps behind them.

'What on earth is going on here?' exclaimed Dr Brown.

***

Arrangements to interview Guy Lombardi had been hastily put in place so that DS Curtis could use the interview facilities at the police station most local to the flat. He was accompanied by Detective Constable Cyril Jones, who was based at the station where they now sat, and who was taking a keen interest in proceedings.

'So, can we just go back a bit?' said DS Curtis, adjusting his position on the uncomfortable plastic interview room chair. 'You are saying that you invested Andrew's money for him in a company involved in the art world, which has gone bust?'

'That is not quite what I said, Detective Sergeant,' Guy was becoming exasperated with the repeated questioning, which had started with the accusation of blackmail, and then moved on to his arrangements with Andrew. 'I said I had made investments in a series of ventures in businesses involved in art dealing and culture, as well as the more usual bank deposits. I thought I had explained that one of the businesses, involved in international art, had ceased trading quite suddenly, and I have not been able to establish what has happened to the money invested...'

'Yes, yes,' said DC Jones. 'And that was the company where you shoved away most of Andrew Gurney's money, correct?'

'A substantial proportion of the proceeds of his more recent sales were invested there, yes, but...'

'And you explained that, in return for this so-called substantial investment, they made you a Director of the company? Surely that must mean you understand what has happened to it, then,' said DS Curtis.

'Unfortunately, not. I had nothing to do with the day-to-day running of the business, and the founder of the company, Christos Georgiou, who is based in Cyprus, has not been taking my calls or answering my emails.' Guy looked from face to face. 'Its all on my phone if you would like to …'

'Don't worry, Mr Lombardi, we will be checking your phone,' said DC Jones. 'But you have only had this particular phone for a couple of weeks, so we probably won't get much. What happened to your previous phone?'

'As I explained to Detective Sergeant Curtis, either I dropped it somewhere, or I had my pocket picked. That is why I got a new one.'

'If you ask me,' said DC Curtis, 'this is what they call a "burner phone" bought to use for nefarious purposes. You can see it is a cheap one. Where is your other phone, Mr Lombardi?'

'Will we discover it when the search warrant comes through and we search the flat?' asked DC Jones.

***

Emma wasn't happy about the arrangement, but seeing as Elliot owned the flat and rented it to her at a substantial discount, in a way, she had no choice.

She got on well enough with Panda in normal times. But these were not normal times, and now that she was helping to carry in the second car-load of clothes, she wondered how long she would be expected to share her flat.

Granted, the second bedroom was only used to store odd bits of furniture, so she had a spare room, but it was *her* flat, and she valued her privacy. Especially since she and Peter ... especially now that she might expect a guest occasionally.

Panda had been very weepy when WPC Linda Hope bought her round, but now that the police woman had departed, she had pulled herself together and got on with the business of moving out of Elliot's house and into her flat.

Emma felt some sympathy for her, of course. She may have been seeing someone else, and there was this blackmail thing, but she was obviously very upset.

When the clothes were unloaded, she suggested that a breath of sea air might do them both good, and persuaded Panda to join her for a short walk along the cliff path, where she ran every morning. They didn't get far before Panda wanted to turn back, explaining that they would soon come up to the wall and the gate at the back of the house she shared with Elliot, and she was not ready to face seeing that yet.

Emma thought she should have gone back there to live, and was a little annoyed that Elliot had effectively dumped Panda on her doorstep. After all, she and Elliot did live in a big house with plenty of space. And then there was her father. He lived in an enormous old place. If she couldn't live with Elliot, why couldn't she go there? And what about the boys, she wondered. How were they taking this?

Obviously, Elliot himself had not taken it well. That was why he had asked Emma to take Panda in.

Poor Elliot. He didn't deserve this, she thought.

***

Three times they had been out with his mates to play darts, and each time she had arranged for her dad to pick her up.

It wasn't that she didn't trust Mikey, it was just that there was still supposed to be this murderer on the lose on the town, and although they could easily walk home from The Nelson, her mum had insisted that her father would pick her up.

It was all right being out with Mikey, even though his mates were a bit leery.

That Johnny was the worst. She knew she wasn't any good at darts, but when it was her turn to throw, he constantly made comments about her chest getting in the way.

They were a nice enough group of lads apart from that, and she knew that it was just the drink talking.

Mikey didn't exactly tell him to leave it, though. She would have liked him to, but he was too much of a lad for that, she supposed.

They had done a bit of snogging before her dad came to pick her up, but she had managed to keep Mikey's hands under control. She wasn't prepared for what he said, though.

'Listen, babe,' he announced. 'I know what you said about being young, and that, but we have been going out for a while now, and …'

'And?'

'And … well, you know.'

'Pardon?'

'Well, I mean, I've spent money buying you drinks and that, and …'

Karen was proud of what she said next.

'And the answer is still no, Mikey. I'm sorry, like, but if you can't deal with that, then you had better find someone else to take along to watch you play darts.'

Chapter 14

'And, before I go, if you don't mind, Panda ... I mean Mrs Markham, I'd like to ask you about your movements on the day of the murder itself,' said Detective Inspector Francis. 'We just need to be clear where everyone was.'

'Yes, I see,' said Panda. 'Well, that was the day Guy, Guy Lombardi, came to value a couple of pictures, up at the farmhouse. I was there to introduce him to my father.'

DS Curtis absorbed this information with interest.

Panda was pretty unconcerned about the risks of introducing her lover to her father, of all people, and inviting him to come to the town where she lived with her husband and children. She must have been very confident in her ability to carry that off. Either that or she had an interest in the proceeds of the pictures if they were sold.

Was this all about money? An idea was growing, and

DS Curtis decided to explore it further.

'And did he take the paintings to be sold?' he asked.

'No,' replied Panda. 'Pop, I mean my father, was interested to hear what he thought they were worth, and increased the insurance on them as a result, I think, but he decided not to sell.'

'How did you feel about that?' asked DI Francis, who had obviously caught on to the same line of thought.

'Feel about it?' asked Panda. 'The potential sale of those pictures, you mean? I can't say it bothered me either way. What my father decides to do with them is not really my concern, although I think the increase in the insurance value helped him to understand their worth a little more. I've always hated those pictures, actually. I don't know if you noticed them when you went to the farm, but they are big dark gloomy things, and when I was a girl, I thought the people in them were miserable.'

***

'But you had been up to the beach huts the day before, Karen?'

'Yeah, and the day before that, after work, like. Me an' Panda went up there to clean 'em up. End of the season, y'see.'

'I see,' said DS Curtis. 'And what exactly does that entail?'

'Well, it's quite easy really, and I get extra money for doing it. Me and Panda got a system, like.'

'A system?'

'Yeah, Panda come up with it before I joined, when she used to do it with Elliot.'

'How does it work?'

'Well, Panda starts at one end, like, and I start at the other. I sweep up all the sand. There is always sand. And I mop the floors and roll up the carpets. Meanwhile Panda wipes everything down, like, checks the furniture, and makes sure the gas bottle is disconnected.'

'Don't you get in each other's way?'

'Nah. That's the clever bit. When we arrive, we open up all the doors and put them on the latch, then when we meet in the middle, we just pass each other and carry on.'

'You meet in the middle?'

'Well, sometimes it's not exactly in the middle, like. But that's when we stop and have a drink and a bit of a breather. It was good we did it when we did this year, 'cos the next day it p..., I mean it rained heavy, like. It's easier to do it if it ain't chucking it down, else we can walk in as much sand as we sweep out.'

'And you put all the doors on the latches as you do this?'

'Yeah, stops locking the keys inside by accident, and lets some air through too.'

'And do you think it might be possible that you left one of the doors on the latch as you finished?'

'What? Not locked, you mean? I don't think so. I doubt it. But I suppose it is possible, like. Why?'

***

Guy sat with his tubby, uncomfortable-looking solicitor, who was sweating slightly, in the windowless interview room. They had agreed beforehand that Guy would try not to lose his temper.

'So you arrived on time for your meeting with Sir Lemuel Fulton-Marks, then Mr Lombardi?'

'Yes. We have been through all this.'

'And what time would that have been, sir?' asked DS Curtis.

'Ten o'clock … look, if you would just take a glance at your notes, all this is in there.'

'Very probably, sir. And did you go straight to the farmhouse, or did you go anywhere else first?'

'No, I told you, I went straight there …'

'Well, that is a little odd, because we have CCTV footage showing your car on the coast road, approaching the town at a little after seven forty-five.'

The solicitor, silent until now, let out a little cough and then subsided.

'Well, that's not right …'

'So you hadn't been to see Stanley Gurney before you went to the meeting at the farm, then?'

'No, I …'

'I warn you, Mr Lombardi, we are discussing a charge of murder here,' said DI Francis. 'So the truth will be your best course of action now, sir, if you don't mind.'

'I don't know what you …'

'I put it to you,' said DI Francis, 'that you drove to Mr Gurney's cottage before you went to the farm. Were you trying to get more of Andrew Gurney's paintings, which may have been kept there?'

'No! That is all wrong! Nothing like that happened, I swear.'

DI Francis ended the interview, and as Guy was led back to his cell, he muttered to DS Curtis that they would let him cool his heels while the seriousness of the situation sank in.

'Just a pity we haven't got a murder weapon, or any idea how Gurney came to be in the beach hut, Curtis.'

'Yes, but I have a theory about that, sir, if you have a moment…'

'Not now, Curtis. I've promised Mrs Francis I will take her to Waitrose, and you wouldn't want to be in my shoes if I missed that!'

**

'Just a courtesy call, really, Mark. I thought you might like to know that the search warrant has come through, and we are going in tomorrow morning, when Andrew Gurney goes over to Dr Brown's place for his therapy session. You are welcome to come along if you are interested.'

'That is excellent news, Cyril,' said DS Curtis. 'I'll be

there, of course. What time are you going in?'

***

Emma pulled the covers up around her ears.

Peter's apartment was quite luxurious compared to hers, with two smart bathrooms and a definite lack of Panda Markham.

Normally, at this time every morning, she would be out on her daily run. But today was very different.

Emma sighed contentedly.

The sound of water running in the en-suite shower soon had her sitting on the edge of the bed, however.

'Would you like me to soap your back, honey?' she called out.

Chapter 15

'Well, yes. I suppose it is possible.' Panda needed to draw on all her amateur dramatics experience now. The questioning was getting dangerously near to the truth.

'You took all the locks on the beach huts off the latch when you finished cleaning,' said DI Francis. 'But you agree that it is conceivable that you could have missed one?'

'I don't think it is very likely, but then, I suppose we were pretty tired. I mean it is quite a physical job …'

'Yes, of course. But as you know, when Emma Johnson discovered the body, the door was on the latch, and she says she did not touch the lock.'

'Didn't the murderer or the victim break in then?'

'I'll be candid with you, Mrs Markham. There are no signs of the door being forced, and unless a key was used, we can't see how he got in, unless the door was left unlocked after you cleaned'

'I see.' There was a pause, and Panda glanced out of the window. It was starting to rain. 'Do you know who did it?'

'Well, yes, I think we do. But can I just ask you about something you said in the flat in London when the discussion turned to the identity of the blackmailer …'

'Go on?'

'According to her notes … ah, yes, here we are … WPC Pope recorded that, when DS Curtis asked if you knew who the blackmailer was, you replied, "I thought I had an idea, but no. I was wrong." Can I ask who you were thinking of at that time?'

Panda felt the bile rising in her throat. They were so close. She had to keep her nerve. She must control this. She must think.

'Well, Andrew admitted that he sent the letter, so …'

'That is not quite what I was asking, Panda … Mrs Markham … Who did you think was blackmailing you before Guy Lombardi incriminated himself?'

She could feel sweat forming between her shoulders. She had to be so careful now. This might ruin everything. They were too close to discovering the mistake she had made about Stanley Gurney blackmailing her. She must not let her fear show.

She must deflect them away from the truth. She must concentrate.

'Emma,' she said. 'I thought it was Emma Johnson, from the office.'

***

They found a painting between the back of the sofa and the wall. It was one of Andrew's earlier works, according to the date neatly painted next to the scrawled signature.

But the odd thing about it, apart from where they found it, was that it was wrapped in a black raincoat. A rather expensive-looking, almost new, raincoat.

Other than that, there was nothing to add further enlightenment in the search.

'Not a sign of his mobile phone?' confirmed DS Curtis. 'His real mobile phone, I mean, not that cheap one he had on him.'

'Sorry, it's not here,' said DC Jones.

'Bugger.'

'Bit odd about that painting wrapped in a mac down the back of the sofa, though …'

'Yes, that is a bit strange,' said DS Curtis. 'Very strange.'

***

Dr Brown went to the door and opened it just a crack.

Waiting on the steps outside was a smartly suited young man holding a large white envelope.

'Yes?' he said.

'Sorry to disturb you. Is this the correct address for a Mr Andrew Gurney?'

'And who might you be?'

'Tim Dent, Folkhard and Driver, Solicitors. I have a letter for Mr Gurney.'

'I could take that ...'

'Thank you, but I am supposed to deliver it to Mr Gurney personally ...'

***

DI Francis did not waste time on preliminaries, and

as soon as Guy, his solicitor and the two detectives were seated, he began.

'So here is what we think happened, Mr Lombardi. You did not drive straight to the meeting at the farmhouse, as you claim. You drove to the car park behind the beach huts near Stanley Gurney's cottage. Then you went to see him and somehow talked him into handing over another of Andrew's pictures before you left.'

'Nonsense ...' said Guy.

'But Stanley Gurney was not happy, and you argued, which resulted in him following you out of the cottage, past the beach huts, as you made your way back to your car with the painting.'

'Oh, honestly, this is too ridiculous ...'

'Outside the beach huts, did he catch you up, sir? Did he perhaps push you into the door of the hut in question, which wasn't properly shut, and which opened?

'This is just supposition,' said the solicitor. 'I think we ...'

'And still arguing, the pair of you went into the beach hut, which is where you stabbed him, isn't it?'

'I ...'

'Where did you hide the weapon, Mr Lombardi?' said DS Curtis. 'You might as well tell us now and save us all the trouble, as we will find it soon enough.'

'And we have a witness who saw you running back to your car,' said DI Francis triumphantly. 'It is time to start telling us the truth now, I think.'

Chapter 16

'I ain't saying I could see who it was, or nuffin',' said Errol Richards. 'I did see a bloke running to a car what was parked up behind the huts. But that's all. My boat was still quite a way offshore when I saw him.'

'Thank you,' said WPC Linda Pope. 'That is very helpful. Now do you understand, Mrs Richards, that you are not to approach Andrew Gurney again or send your lawyer round to his apartment. The wording of this Restraining Order is very clear.'

***

'Yes, all right, I admit I did go to the cottage before I went to the farmhouse. But I didn't see Andrew's father, at least not to speak to.'

'But you did see him, Mr Lombardi?'

'Yes, he was down by his boat working on something.'

'So you waited for him?'

'No. Look, do I have to …'

'Just explain what happened as we discussed,' said the solicitor.

'OK. All right then, if I must.' Guy sighed and put his hands, palm down, on the interview room table. 'I could see Gurney, but I didn't think he had seen me. The front door of the cottage was open, you see. It opens straight into the sitting room.'

'Go on,' said DS Curtis.

'Well, I knew the painting was on the wall just inside the sitting room, so I stepped in …' Guy seemed to deflate a little and looked at his lawyer, who nodded and indicated that he should continue.

'And then what?'

'Well, I don't know what came over me really, but I reached up and unhooked the painting.'

'And ran off with it?'

'Well, I … Yes. Andrew asked me to collect it, you see, and I was going to be late for my meeting, so …'

'That is not true, is it, Guy. Andrew was surprised to see the painting when we showed it to him in the flat, and he asked what it was doing there. He told us he had given it to his father,' DS Curtis paused to draw breath. 'It is one of the series of his paintings that were shown on the local TV news some years ago, when Andrew's talent first emerged.'

'That is why you snatched it, isn't it? Had you already got a buyer lined up?' said DI Francis.

Guy looked pleadingly at his lawyer, but made no reply.

'And then, as you ran off, Stan Gurney saw you and gave chase. He caught up with you at the beach huts, and that is where you murdered him, isn't it?'

DI Francis looked at DS Curtis and nodded.

DS Curtis got to his feet and said, 'Guy Lombardi, I am arresting you for the murder of Stanley Gurney. You do not have to say anything, but ...'

Guy looked up to the ceiling, threw back his head and yelled 'NO!' at the top of his voice.

Chapter 17

'So, just to be clear,' said DI Francis. 'What did you do after the meeting with your father. You said you left the farm at the same time as Guy, I think ...'

'Oh. Yes. Well. Um ...'

'Panda?'

'Look, I'm not proud of my behaviour with Guy, but ... well, we had a very physical relationship and after the meeting we ...'

'Yes?'

'Do you want me to draw you a picture? Isn't it obvious? We went back to my house.'

'Nobody was at home?'

'We didn't have an audience, if that is what you mean.'

'I'm sorry, I didn't mean to be indiscreet. I meant the boys were at school and Elliot was at work.'

'Yes. I hope we can change the subject now.'

***

'Yes, they are through here, Detective Inspector.'

'Thank you, Sir Lemuel. I was passing, and I just thought I would drop in and see your pictures myself, to see what Guy Lombardi was interested in here. Do you mind?'

'Not at all. Not at all. By this time of day, I've usually had enough out on the farm, so I tend to sneak back up here for a cup of tea and a sit down. It is lucky you caught me. Age catches up with one, y'know.'

'I hope it is no trouble.'

'No, no trouble. You will join me in a cup of tea, of course.'

'Thank you very much, sir.'

'Right, well here they are then. These pictures were acquired out in Africa somewhere, by my grandfather, so the story goes. Never been terribly fond of them myself. Bunch of miserable-looking coves, if you ask me. They look like they would slit your throat as soon as look at you.'

'Native warriors in war dress?'

'Zulu, actually. Supposed to be very tall, I'm told. Wouldn't like to meet one of them on a dark night, especially carrying all those weapons and whatnot.'

'No, sir. Very daunting.'

'By the by, have you found the murder weapon yet? I was chatting to the chaps about it down at the cricket club, shortly after it happened, when the details came out in the paper …'

'An unfortunate thing, that. I've no idea where they got so much detail …'

'Probably from the ambulance people who mopped him up. Those I met at the opening of the new ambulance station were incorrigible chatterboxes.'

'Really? Well, that's interesting …'

'Anyway, this thing about the weapon. Tiny entry wound. Almost surgical, and deep penetration. Sounded to me like a Zulu assegai, like that chap on the right of the picture is holding. They use them as thrusting blades. Sort of short spears that you hold, rather than throw. I've got one of those. Like to see it?'

They moved back to the spacious main hall, and Sir Lemuel opened the cabinet by the fireplace and reached up to the top shelf.

'It is up here somewhere ... Ah, here we are. See that knob on the bottom? That is where you place the palm of your hand and thrust upwards, see?'

Force of habit made DI Francis take the weapon between finger tip and thumb.

'Vicious-looking thing,' he said.

'Yes, and pretty much no thicker than my fountain pen. You can see how that would only make a small entry wound and penetrate deep. One of the Zulu words for these things is "Iklwa". Apparently, that refers to the noise it makes when you withdraw it from your victim. Graphic, eh?'

'Yuk!' DI Francis turned the implement gently between his fingers and looked at the point where the wooden shaft joined the blade.

'How old is this thing?' he asked, handing it back.

'Well, it must be over a hundred years, I suppose. No use to anybody now, and of no real monetary value. My father used it and the other African stuff in the collection up there to scare us silly with gory bedtime stories.' Sir Lemuel chuckled at the memory.

'Nasty looking thing, and I see what you mean, likening it to the murder weapon. But we think it was one of those horrible 'zombie knives' you can buy on the internet. We sometimes confiscate those from kids, even around here. They are not just confined to the cities.'

'Indeed so. Tea?'

***

Dr Brown was surprised by how well the introduction went.

Lena was not as young as some of the others he had interviewed and had done similar work before, both in London and in her native Poland. She spoke excellent English and had some good qualifications.

The big question, however, was whether Andrew would accept her.

'Was no need to worry,' said Lena, on the steps on the way out. 'He seem sweet boy, and we have maybe the connection already.'

'I think you may be right, Lena. Would you be interested in the position?' Dr Brown said.

It would take a week or ten days to sort out all the arrangements and get Lena moved into what was Guy's bedroom, and 'live-in' care like this was not going to be cheap. But at least when it was in place, it would give Dr Brown some of his life back, and that was a bonus.

Andrew was used to being on his own when Guy went to work, but could not cook, clean or shop at all, and could not be left alone at night.

Dr Brown was at pains to warn her to watch out for the signs of one of Andrew's obsessive periods coming on. They occurred particularly as he was finishing a painting, and there had been occasions when he could not be convinced to rest, working for marathon sessions and forgetting to eat or drink. The record was fifty-two hours straight, during which he and Guy took it in turns to encourage, cajole, and sometimes almost force him to take sustenance and rest.

Lena had at least worked with such a case previously, although he was an old man and passed away a couple of years after she took him on. In explaining the situation then, she produced highly relevant examples of exactly this type of behaviour, and Dr Brown was very encouraged. He was confident that she could cope and that, if Andrew would accept her, a solution had been found.

During the few days after the interview, Andrew often asked about Lena and actually said he was looking forward to her moving in.

Dr Brown was delighted.

***

It happened on the evening they went ten-pin bowling.

Mikey was supposed to be giving a lift to one of his mates, so Karen felt happy enough to accept his offer to go along. Until the mate cried off with a stomach upset, and she and Mikey were alone in the car, everything was fine.

There was a little harmless cuddling when they arrived at the venue, but on the way home after Mikey had a few drinks, things got more serious.

Karen was not used to strong cider, but when the lager ran out, that was what Mikey bought her. She should have stuck to Pepsi.

Mikey pulled into a deserted car park on the edge of an industrial estate, and she happily went along with the kissing for a while, but then it got a bit out of hand.

Mikey somehow got her seat to go back and had her top up and her bra undone in a trice. Then, while she didn't actually ask him to in as many words, he just didn't stop, and she couldn't keep on pushing away his strong hands undoing her jeans.

When it was over, he apologised, dropped the prophylactic out of the car window, and begged for her forgiveness. Karen realised she had left her virginity on the tarmac of an industrial estate's car park.

But despite it all, she had forgiven him. Then they did it again, and this time Mikey was much more gentle, and she relaxed. When he finished this time, she was beginning to enjoy it. And when he told her he loved her, she said she loved him too.

Chapter 18

Of course, because he owned it, Elliot still had a key to Emma's flat, although he sat outside in his car until he saw her setting off for her morning run.

Emma was a creature of habit and took off for a run every morning at this time without fail, come rain or shine, and following her usual route. So Elliot knew when she was likely to be out.

From what Emma had told him, Panda just slopped about the flat in her dressing gown these days and sat on the sofa, under the quilt from her bed, watching reruns of old American soap operas since moving in, so Elliot expected her to be at home.

He was not disappointed.

He did not bother to knock, but just let himself into the flat, and there, in the lounge, he found Panda, bathed in sunlight streaming in from the kitchen window behind her.

'Elliot?' she stammered as he walked in.

'Who were you expecting? One of your other boyfriends?'

Elliot reached forward, grabbed the quilt from over her knees and yanked it aside. In a moment, he had bunched the hair on the back of her head in his fist and pulled her roughly to her feet.

Her screech of shock and pain did not deter him, and, ignoring her flailing arms, as her towelling dressing gown fell open, he began walking her backwards towards the kitchen.

'I'm going to teach you such a lesson, Panda,' he snarled, pushing her onward towards the solid old table under the window.

Still holding her hair, with his free hand, he pulled the gown free of her shoulders, and it dropped to the floor, where it became entangled around her feet, and she began to stumble and lose her balance.

Now wearing just a pair of knickers, she cried out again.

'Elliot! No. Please stop this!'

In trying to prevent herself from falling, she turned slightly towards the table, and Elliot assisted her action with a firm shove, which saw her fall across the table, face down.

Elliot was growling like a wild animal now.

'You sly little bitch. How dare you? I'm going to make you sorry …'

Elliot adjusted his grip so that he now held her by the back of the neck with one hand, and he ground her face into the wood. With his other hand, he caught hold of the belt on his trousers and released the buckle.

'Please, you are hurting me …'

'Good.'

'What are you going to do? Please … stop!'

As his trousers fell to just above his knees, Elliot kicked out at Panda's leg, forcing her to struggle for balance again and stand with her legs further apart.

Now he pulled back a little and viciously ripped her knickers aside.

At the second attempt, the fabric gave way, and now he pushed her torso down onto the hard table, immobilising her by using his hands to grip her biceps from behind.

Now that she realised what he was going to do, Panda started to sob.

'No, No! Please stop … Oh please don't do this …

please!'

With a grunt, he removed one hand and prepared himself with it. Then, grabbing, bunching and pulling hard on her hair again, he smashed her face into the table top and lunged forward.

Through a mouth full of blood, Panda pleaded.

'No! No! Not … Not that, I don't … Ow! Stop it. You are hurting me … STOP!'

'Shut up, you filthy, dirty little bitch. You will take your punishment. You belong to me!' and he lifted her head and rammed her face into the table once more.

***

Emma could hear noises from the hall, and she rushed to open the front door.

She was temporarily dazzled by the sun straming through the kitchen window, and for a moment she could not see what what was going on.

She could see the shape of a man who had his back to her, in the kitchen, at the table, and she could hear, rather than see Panda's distress. It was quickly obvious what was happening, and Panda's repeated cries galvanised her into action.

She reached out blindly, grabbing a knife from the wooden block by the hob and stepping forward, just as the grunting man drew back.

She had not meant to cut him, but the combined force of their collision made it inevitable.

The blood spurted from his neck, and she realised with horror that she had stabbed into his carotid artery.

The moment of recognition came as the man grabbed his neck in a futile attempt to stem the pulsing blood.

'Elliot?' said Emma, as the knife clattered onto the floor. 'Oh God, no!'

***

The blood on her fingers made getting her mobile phone out of her 'Armpocket' and dialling the number difficult, but eventually Emma managed to summon an ambulance.

Panda had passed out as soon as the blood began to spurt from Elliot's neck, and her head hit the floor with a slap as she landed, and slid under the table in front of his twitching body.

Emma tried shoving Panda's limp form aside to get to Elliot and searched desperately in her memory for what to do. She remembered something about applying pressure to stem the bleeding, but where should she press?

She tried pushing her fingers above and below the cut, but there was so much blood, and it made everything so slippery, that she could not get a purchase on anything.

Elliott's eyes were rolling now, and his arms were flailing, as he made gurgling noises through the bubbling saliva coming from his mouth.

'Help me ...' he whispered.

Emma felt waves of nausea washing over her. She must not pass out, she must not. She must help in some way. But her last conscious thought was that she was falling and colliding with Elliott's exposed genitals as her head fell onto his now prostrate body.

Chapter 19

'So do you think that Emma was another one having an affair with Randy Panda, and she killed Elliot out of jealousy?'

'A lesbian thing, you mean, sir?'

'Well, anything is possible, and seems to be allowed nowadays, so who knows,' said DI Francis.

'That doesn't seem right somehow, sir,' said DS Curtis. 'I'm thinking maybe Elliot and Panda were, as it were, making up after he threw her out. Maybe that was how they liked it. Although maybe then he got too angry and it got out of hand, judging by the damage to her face.'

'But why was Emma there then, and if we assume it was her who slashed his neck, why did she do it?'

'Not a clue, sir. And I don't think we will be getting much from Panda or Emma until the sedation wears off.'

'No, I suppose not. It is possible that Panda is not

aware that Elliot has died, Curtis, so you had better get a WPC round here to be by her bed when she comes round.'

'What about Emma, sir. We have to assume she is the murderer, don't we?'

'Yes, and she could be dangerous when she comes round. Now I come to think of it, let's not forget that Panda originally thought that Emma was the blackmailer. It is possible that it has some bearing … Perhaps restraining straps would be a good idea.'

'I ask the duty nurse to organise it, sir.'

***

The search warrant for Emma's flat came through amazingly quickly this time, and DS Curtis met the forensic team there.

There was nothing much unexpected to find, except some possibly elderly rodent droppings in a corner of the kitchen, under a unit, and until they began to explore Panda's clothes in the wardrobe, the search had been fruitless.

Panda had a huge collection of clothes, which spilt out from the wardrobe onto the bedside tables, dressing table and a low chair in the bedroom. Going through this lot would take some time, and

DS Curtis was about to excuse himself when one of the officers picked up an orange T-shirt with what appeared to be a slight stain on the left-hand side.

The officer examined the garment and a pair of jeans, which were bundled up with it in an uncharacteristically untidy way. The rest of the clothes were all ironed and neatly folded, or on hangers, but these two had been hastily wrapped around each other and cast aside, by the look of things.

DS Curtis noticed a small bulge in the back pocket of the jeans and asked the technician to see what it was.

Using infinite care, the officer soon had a strip of screwed-up sellotape and a small twist of what looked like old brown leather in his blue-gloved hand.

***

Lena and Dr Brown held an informal 'case conference' in the consulting rooms once a week.

'Is going well, I thinking. Andrew is quite relax with me, now I learn his routines.'

'That is excellent, Lena. But what about you? How

are you coping with living there? Is there anything you need?'

'No, is fine. Thank you, Doctor. Only one thing, we need more sketch pads. Andrew is now bring me sketches most mornings.'

'Well, that is interesting. Sketches of what?'

'Is ladies, or bits of ladies. He trying to draw a lady from the back. He struggling to get shoulders right, he say. Is just head and the shoulders sketches.'

'I see. Well, I can tell you that Andrew has always felt that he is not much good at painting people, and usually they are just indistinct smears in his pictures. If he is having a go at portraiture, that is a new departure.'

'I'm thinking, yes. But is odd he paint them from the back, not the face.'

'I have no explanation for that one, Lena. So long as it is not making him get too frustrated, I'm sure it will be fine.'

'And you order the sketch pads?'

'I will do it straight away.'

***

Parking their car on the drive, DS Curtis and DI Francis arrived as Sir Lemuel drew up in a Land Rover, coming from one of the tracks leading out to the farm.

'Hello there. Glad to see you again, and so on and so forth, but at a bit of a loss as to what is so urgent after our last meeting earlier today. Has anything changed with Panda's health?' said Sir Lemuel.

'I'm very sorry to have to disturb you again, sir,' said DI Francis, 'and there is no change. But Detective Sergeant Curtis … I mean, we have a theory about something that you may be able to help us with.'

'Happy to help, of course. Shall we go inside?'

'I wonder,' said DS Curtis now, 'If we might examine that Zulu spear thing again, sir …'

'The 'iklwa'? Yes, if you like. Let me get it down for you.'

'No, if it is all the same to you, would you mind if we got it down, sir?' said DS Curtis, pulling on a set of blue vinyl gloves and stepping towards the display cabinet.

'As you please … can I ask what the idea is here?'

DS Curtis gently teased the weapon out from its

resting place and set it on the large hall table.

He indicated the band of what looked like dried animal skin where the handle met the blade, and turning it over carefully, he noticed that part of the binding was missing.

'What happened here?' he asked.

'No idea. Old age, probably, that must be at least a hundred years old …'

'Would you mind if we borrowed this implement, Sir Lemuel? I would like to show it to the forensic boys working on the case.'

'And just one question, if you wouldn't mind before we go, Sir Lemuel,' said DI Francis. 'When he visited to evaluate your paintings, was that the only time Guy Lombardi came here, and was he ever left alone in this hallway?'

Sir Lemuel chuckled.

'I make that two questions, Detective Inspector, but no, he only visited once as far as I'm aware. And I met him on the doorstep and took him straight in to see the pictures. After that, he left with Panda, if I remember correctly.'

Things moved quickly after that.

Because the forensic team were still looking at

Emma and Panda's flat, DI Francis was able to get them to take the weapon and include it in the lab studies.

'And if you find that bit of leather, or whatever it is matches the stuff securing the handle to the blade, please let us know immediately,' said DS Curtis.

***

Two days later, they had their answer.

The small stain on the T-shirt was blood, and the sellotape was definitely from the envelope containing Andrew's letter sent to her father, which Panda had put in her pocket.

There were no useful fingerprints, but there were microscopic traces of blood on the weapon. Could they match those on the T-shirt, and were they the same blood group as Stanley Gurney?

"We have some more work to do to see if there is a DNA match on the blood," read the email from the forensic team. "But the piece of animal skin, subject to all the usual caveats, may well have come from the binding on the weapon. It has obviously been through a washing machine recently, so more testing is needed to be certain of an exact match, but it certainly looks like a *potential* match."

DS Curtis printed off the email and went to see DI Francis.

'Excuse me, sir,' he said as he approached the desk in the untidy open-plan office, 'But I think we have a murder weapon, and there is now some doubt that the murderer is the person we currently have in custody.'

Chapter 20

If it wasn't Guy, then the facts pointed to Stan Gurney's murderer being either Sir Lemuel, Panda, or her brother.

Panda's brother could be discounted pretty much immediately. Whilst he knew of the existence of the 'iklwa', he lived in a house right over on the other side of the farm and claimed he had not seen the weapon since childhood. He also had a cast-iron alibi for the time of the murder and witnesses, in the form of two farmworkers, who could confirm his whereabouts.

Arguably, if you accepted the timeline, he was with Sir Lemuel at the farm when the murder took place, and the pair couldn't be in two places at once.

That left Panda.

And if it was Panda, and the circumstantial evidence strongly suggested it was, how did she do it?

The timeline did not fit. Sir Lemuel said she had arrived at the farm shortly before the meeting with

Guy when, they assumed, she spotted Andrew's letter amongst the post and concealed it in her back pocket.

Before the meeting, she was at home, she said, getting the boys ready for school, or on her way to the meeting with Guy at the farm. And after the meeting, she was with Guy at her house.

Guy had seen Stanley Gurney, very much alive, before the meeting, when he went to steal the painting, and until now, they had been convinced that an altercation outside the beach huts led to the murder taking place there. They had a witness who saw Guy leaving, or should that be that he *thought* he saw him leaving.

DS Curtis scratched his head. They were missing something. But what was it?

Guy had not been alone in the hall and may not even have known of the existence of the 'iklwa'.

There was no time for Panda to have got the 'iklwa' from the cabinet before the meeting with Guy, and she was never on her own in the hall, according to her father, before the meeting anyway. And she left with Guy straight afterwards.

She was apparently at home with Elliot, getting the boys up before that.

Unfortunately, however, Elliot, the one person who

could confirm that, was dead.

What if Panda already had the weapon in her possession before the meeting with Guy? And if that was right, how and when did she get it back into the collection in the display case?

Supposing the 'time of death' estimate was wrong and Stanley Gurney was murdered after the meeting at the farm? That would cast doubt on Guy and Panda's alibi as to what they did after the meeting. But that was several hours after the Coroner's estimate, and the 'time of death' in these cases was never usually that inaccurate.

Perhaps they returned to the beach and murdered Stanley together. But then, how did Errol's sighting of a person, presumably Guy, running away towards his car and driving out of the car park before the meeting at the farm fit in? And then there was the problem of how the weapon got back in the collection cabinet again.

Perhaps Panda murdered Stanley Gurney on her own.

The lack of fingerprints on the weapon made it difficult to prove. Perhaps the DNA analysis would help, but the results of that were some time away.

But then there was the blood on Panda's tee-shirt, and the scrap of animal skin binding in her pocket.

Panda was slightly built. Would she have had the strength to push the blade deep into the victim's abdomen and up into his heart? And when could she have done it?

And what about Emma? Why had she killed Elliot? What was that all about?

***

Panda came round first and had to be told that her husband had been murdered.

She may have been unfaithful to him, but she was very fond of him and realised that he had provided the security and the comfortable life she had enjoyed. He was also the father of her two beautiful boys.

When she thought of the boys, she became distraught and had to be sedated again, albeit mildly this time.

When Emma came round, she was horrified to find herself strapped to a bed in an isolation ward with a policeman outside the door.

They thought she was a murderer. And when the full horror of what she had done hit her, she screamed until she could scream no more.

***

When Sir Lemuel first learned of his son-in-law's death and the trauma his daughter had suffered, he drove straight to the hospital, and he was at her side as soon as the news of Elliot's death was revealed to her.

After a distressing time spent trying to comfort her, he stepped out into the corridor and called the family solicitor, who promised to be with them inside an hour.

On the telephone, he explained that this situation was going to get nasty, and getting it under control was going to take some time.

He squared his shoulders and walked back into the hospital room, where Panda had fallen into a deep sleep.

He suggested that the WPC beside Panda's bed might like to take five minutes and get a coffee or something, and volunteered to stay with his daughter.

As the WPC closed the door, Sir Lemuel looked closely at his sleeping daughter.

'Did you kill old Stan Gurney?' he whispered. 'Could

you have done that?'

Chapter 21

By the third time the police officers took Emma through the sequence of events leading up to Elliot's death, she had managed to regain some control, and her tears had dried up.

They told her that Panda had said Elliot had broken her nose, so they understood that Emma stumbled on the scene in the flat but did not initiate it, and they accepted her statement about how she came to pick up the knife.

But she was still strapped to the bed, so her eyes were wiped by a nurse as DS Curtis read her rights and arrested her for the manslaughter of Elliot Markham. At least she wasn't being charged with murder.

Whilst the policeman seemed to accept that it was an accident, and Emma took some comfort in that, every time she closed her eyes, she saw all that blood again, and she had to fight down the panic once more.

When the nurse returned to offer her a drink through a straw, she asked how Panda was. She was relieved to hear that, although somewhat bruised, especially around her face and jaw, and with a badly a broken nose, Panda was 'comfortable' and expected to make a full recovery.

As for the state of her mind after the horrendous incidents of the last few days, it was too early to say.

***

Jim Pike had been working as a Postman for nearly forty years, he stated. He had been walking up that long drive and delivering to the farmhouse for the best part of twenty-five of those years, and he was looking forward to his retirement.

When Sir Lemuel asked him how the post came to be on the big table in the hall, he had answered that he had not put it there, and that he would never go into a house uninvited. That, he stated, was what letterboxes were for, although he wished sometimes that people would put them at the other end of their long drives to make a postman's job easier.

But, he remembered quite clearly that he had met little Panda on the drive that day and given the letters to her. Of course, she was a grown woman now, but he remembered seeing her up at the farm when she was just a small girl. Back then, he often met her playing on the drive, riding her little pink bike with the basket on the front. He used to give her the letters to take in, back in those days, as well. Sweet little girl, she was.

He wouldn't have thought anything about it, he said, if he hadn't seen that thing in the paper this morning about the progress with the murder enquiry, and how the police had found the murder weapon up at the farmhouse. He remembered that that day was his grandson's birthday, so he was up there earlier than usual to get done and get round to see the lad.

Panda had offered to take the letters in for him when he met her on the drive.

When Postman Jim Pike worked out what time he had delivered to the farmhouse, by working backwards from when he finished his round, another piece of the jigsaw fell into place for DS Curtis, and with the notes from his telephone conversation in his hand, he went to seek out DI Francis.

***

Emma was taken into custody and delivered to a chilly, bare cell in a noisy corridor.

Manslaughter was not to be taken lightly as a crime, and the arrangements for the detention of suspects pending an initial Court appearance were not intended to be luxurious.

She had a visit from the solicitor Peter found for her. With Elliot gone and Panda too closely involved, she could not think who else to ask to help her, but Peter had stepped up and been marvellous.

He seemed to know his way around the system and soon arranged for her to receive her first visit from a lawyer.

The imposing figure before her now turned out to be none other than the Senior Partner of Mansell Bower, an up-market, multi-disciplinary law firm that she had actually heard of.

But his presence did nothing to help her to relax, and she struggled to contain her panic and think more clearly about the situation she found herself in.

The solicitor explained confidently that it was likely that 'the incident', as he called it, would soon be recognised as an accident and she would be free to go. She hoped he was right.

The slight problem, the solicitor stated, was that Emma had picked up a knife when she entered the kitchen. They would have to be able to prove that she did it to defend herself rather than to cause harm to the attacker.

In Emma's mind, she repeatedly asked herself the same question. How on earth could she prove it?

And if she could not, was she destined to spend years in prison for her actions.

***

Karen had only recently been entrusted with a key to the office, and she felt the responsibility keenly.

When she unlocked the door to open up the business, and nobody else turned up, she was surprised to find that she was alone.

Uncertain what else to do, she had just put the kettle on when WPC Linda Pope came through the door.

Chapter 22

This was to be the third meeting Dr Brown had had with the solicitor appointed to find Andrew's money, and this time there was better news.

Apparently, once Guy Lombardi had learned that the charge of murder against him was being dropped, he became very much more cooperative, and while he still faced serious charges of fraud and theft, he offered the lawyers good information about what he had done.

A modest amount of Andrew's money was in a straightforward current account with a High Street bank, and that, the lawyer stated, could be used to defray immediate costs without too much difficulty.

They had also identified several small accounts and two quite substantial accounts, with a Building Society, in Guy's name. Proceedings had been instigated to have them turned over to a central holding account, to be administered by Guy's lawyer, and held in trust.

The company Guy was a Director of, which had suddenly ceased trading, was a more intractable problem, the lawyer explained. But some progress had been made to identify those involved at least.

There was also news that His Majesty's Revenue and Customs had declared an interest in some unpaid tax on a string of transactions involving international art trading, where it appeared Guy had invested funds in some highly dubious artwork sales abroad.

There may be a way to go, the lawyer explained, but at least they were lifting the lid on the tangled web of Guy's financial exploits, and enough money had been found to cover the initial costs of sorting it all out.

***

They knew that dropping the murder charge against Guy Lombardi would soon get picked up by the press, but it could not be avoided.

At least he was remanded in custody for the fraud, and thanks to the input from HMRC as to tax owed here and abroad, they were able to convince a judge that Guy was a flight risk, and they should keep him under lock and key. For the time being, at least.

But now the pressure was on to resolve the murder of Stanley Gurney, and they were clutching at straws.

***

'May I speak to Chief Constable Henry Barton-Mills, please? ... eh? ... what? Oh, ah, Fulton-Marks is the name.'

'Lemmy! How the devil are you?'

'Barty, old lad ...'

'Absolutely fine, old man! I was going to give you a call ...'

'Well, yes. Look, the thing is, Barty, old sport, I ...'

'Awful news about young Elliot. I was very sorry to hear that. He was a good sort, for an estate agent.'

'Yes, well. About that ...'

'How is Panda bearing up? Must be devastated ...'

'Look here, Barty, will you switch from broadcast to receive for a second, and let a fellow catch his breath. I might have some important information for you.'

'Sorry, Lemmy. Say on. Say on!'

'It's about our local postman …'

'Your postman, Lemmy? Is this not something for your local Community Action …'

'Hush, Barty. Hear me out. It could be important.'

***

Panda expressed a wish to go home and be with her boys.

Her brother and his wife had taken them in and were prepared to offer to accommodate Panda too, if she could not face going back to the home she shared with Elliot quite yet. It was decided she would stay with them to convalesce for a while before any decisions were made about the future.

Eventually, her father convinced her to stay in the private hospital adjacent to the NHS hospital she was in now, for a couple of days beforehand, to let the injuries and the severe bruising, to her face in particular, heal a little.

'Not to put too fine a point on it, Panda, old girl, you currently look like Frankenstein's monster, and you will scare the boys to death,' he said.

***

After the two detectives interviewed the postman, Jim Pike, at the insistence of the Chief Constable, some anomalies with the timeline came into sharp focus.

They interviewed Panda again, this time in the private hospital, in light of the new information.

'Did you go down to the beach huts early in the morning with Guy before the meeting at the farmhouse, Mrs Markham?' asked DI Francis.

'How could I have done? I took the boys to school, then went to the farm to collect their birthday bikes and take them home. You know all this. After that, I went back to the farm for the meeting with Guy.'

'What did you do in the period between collecting the bikes and going back to the farm?'

'We have been through all this, Inspector,' Panda scowled. 'I told you I took the bikes home, struggled to get them into the mower shed, had a coffee, used the bathroom, changed and went to the meeting with Guy.'

'You didn't go anywhere else before the meeting, after you took the boys to school?' asked DS Curtis.

'No.'

Something was nagging at DS Curtis about the timeline again. But now they had to challenge Panda about her visit to the farmhouse.

'We have a statement from the local postman to say that he handed the post to you on the driveway and you took it into the house,' said DI Francis. 'Do you remember that?'

'The postman?' Panda felt the hairs on the back of her neck begin to stand up. If they knew about the postman, they might be able to work out when she was at the farmhouse the first time. She composed herself and, reminding herself of her days with the amateur dramatic group, got into character.

'What postman?' she said.

'The same postman who has been delivering to the farm for over twenty years.'

'Old Jim?' she said. 'Is he still around?'

'You don't recall him handing you the post on the morning of the meeting?'

'He might have done. I don't recall.'

'Can we go back a bit, please?' said DS Curtis. 'Just remind me about your arrangement to do the end of season clean of the beach huts.'

'This again?' Panda sighed. 'Is this really going to help you catch this murderer?'

'It might. Indulge me.'

Panda shrugged.

'You explained that you took all the locks on the beach huts off the latch when you finished cleaning. But you agreed that it was conceivable that you could have missed one?'

'I suppose it could have happened. You told me there was no sign of a break-in.'

'That's right. And you finished the cleaning with Karen the night before the murder took place.'

'Yes, that's right.'

'Where were all the keys when you finished?'

'In my …' Panda caught herself. 'I took them back to the office.'

'When did you take them back to the office, Mrs Markham?'

'I told you. When we finished the cleaning.'

At that moment, a nurse arrived with tea for the patient and said pointedly that visiting hours were displayed in the foyer.

'OK, I'm sorry, nurse. We have finished here,' said DI Francis. 'Thank you, Panda.'

Out in the carpark DI Francis looked at DS Curtis as he unlocked the car.

'What the hell was all that about cleaning the beach huts, Mark?'

'I think we might need to interview Karen, the office junior, again,' he replied.

Chapter 23

'I don't think so,' said Peter, in response to Emma's question.

Asking if she could temporarily move into his flat rather than her own, while hers was redecorated, when she was eventually released, seemed such a little thing to ask, now that they were lovers.

'I trust you will find the solicitor I introduced you to satisfactory. He has a terrific reputation,' Peter was saying. 'I gave him your address to send the bills.'

'I ... I thought ...' stammered Emma into the phone.

'I'd better be going,' said Peter. 'I'll probably see you around sometime, maybe at yoga, when this is over.'

And he was gone.

Thinking about it afterwards, she supposed she should not be surprised. She imagined that having a girlfriend who stood accused of manslaughter might not be good for his career. And Government Officials were strict about that sort of thing.

***

Even now, three weeks later, every time she closed her eyes, she could see all that blood again. And as for sleeping, the dreams meant she didn't dare.

Emma found herself actively trying to avoid going to sleep.

In a way, she wished that the hearing had not resulted in her being granted bail and allowed to go home. At least in the prison cell, the constant noise would blot out her thoughts. When she was first released, she could not bring herself to go back to the flat, so she booked herself into one of the shabby hotels down by the seafront.
There she suffered a recurring nightmare whenever she dared to close her eyes, and the lack of sleep gave her a persistent headache.

Fortunately, she was naturally quite an organised person, and despite her grief and discomfort, she threw herself into the tasks that came next. That did at least give her some respite from the painful thoughts which surrounded her.

She hired a firm of 'forensic cleaners' who were specialists in cleaning up properties where 'incidents', as they called them, had occurred. She found them thanks to a tip from WPC Linda Pope, and she gave them a week to scour her flat clean. They also bagged up all Panda's clothes and effects from the bedroom she had used and delivered them to her brother's house.

Each of the string of contractors she hired next had to come to the hotel to collect and return the key. She could not face going to the flat, even just to unlock the door.

She found and employed a team of decorators to paint everything white, and as the 'forensic cleaners' had removed the floor coverings in the kitchen, she followed that by having new vinyl flooring laid. And finally, she arranged to get all of the carpets cleaned in the whole flat.

The process took three full weeks, and to get the tradesmen there quickly, she was aware that she probably overpaid, but that didn't matter. It had to be done.

During the time the work was going on, she found a vacant holiday caravan on a big site near the sea. The owner agreed to rent it to her for three months in return for a sizeable pile of cash. Out of season, such properties often sat empty, so the owner was probably delighted. The rent worked out to be a little more than she had been paying Elliot for an entire two-bedroom flat in a good location, but he had given her a very generous discount on the rent. The static caravan was pretty grotty, and as it seemed she was the only person staying on the site, she doubted if the owner was actually allowed to let it this time of year. But it would have to do, and it was better than the hotel.

In the hotel, she would sit up watching awful American soap operas or even endless repeats of the 'twenty-four-hour news', just to fight off the urge to sleep. And if she felt herself dozing, she would stand up behind the solitary armchair and watch the flickering hotel TV from there.

When she did fall asleep, the nightmare was always the same, and she woke up bathed in sweat.

Even in the daytime, she thought about Elliot and the boys, without a father because of her, and she frequently found herself weeping. Time hung heavy on her hands, and she wondered if she would ever feel right again.

Why, oh why, had she picked up that kitchen knife? If she had not done that, none of this would have happened.

In desperation, she went to see the doctor. Perhaps she was becoming paranoid, but she got the impression that he was just going through the motions and holding her at arm's length. She needed help, but she was sure he just wanted to process her and send her on her way. He knew who she was, of course, and what had happened, but with a prescription for pills to help her sleep in her hand, she felt as though she was being dismissed.

***

The sketch Andrew presented this morning had much more detail.

Andrew's paintings and drawings were very precise, and his style had been described as 'uncannily accurate' and in the 'photorealism' mode. The more excitable press compared his work to that of the American Richard Estes, or perhaps, when discussing his larger landscapes and his mastery of perspective, to Canaletto.

Today's offering was more than slightly disconcerting to Lena.

There was her bedroom, as seen from the lounge door, with the curtains roughly pulled across the window, and her bedclothes in some disarray. The detail, although this was only a pencil sketch, was remarkable.

But what was really breathtaking was what was on her bed.

A shapely naked female form, viewed from the back, knelt astride a very obviously male lover. His position, face up with his legs spread apart, left no uncertainty as to what this couple were doing and left little to the imagination.

Lena gasped and dropped the sketchpad on the kitchen worktop.

'What is meaning, Andrew? This is dirt!'

'Dirt?' said Andrew, confused. 'I want to know if I've got them right. Do they look realistic?'

'Too bladdy realistic, Andrew! Is pornography! Is not right, draw this, you get in trouble.'

'In trouble? I don't understand. I know it is not quite right yet, but I think it is the best I've done so far. That is what they looked like to me.'

'What who looked? Is my bedroom, no? Nothing like that happening there!'

'But it did. That is Guy and Panda Markham, just before the telephone rang and spoiled it.'

***

'Do you like wanna cup of tea?' asked Karen as they sat on the client chairs in the estate agent's office. 'It's about all I can actually do here, I dunno what to say when people come in, or nuffin.'

'Perhaps it would be better if you were to close the office for the time being, at least until Emma gets back. You could put a notice in the window,' said DI Francis. 'Temporary closure due to family bereavement, or something.'

'I dunno how to spell "bereavement".'

'I'll write it down for you.'

'Karen,' said DS Curtis, 'When you and Panda finished cleaning the beach huts, what did you do with all the keys?'

'I dunno … no, wait. Panda put 'em in her glove box, in the car.'

'Did she take them straight back to the office?'

'I … I'm not sure. No hold on … We was well tired when we finished, like, and a bit grubby, so she says she was going home to have a shower, and the keys would be safe enough in there, and like she could take 'em back in the morning.'

'Thank you, Karen, that is very helpful.'

'I can't promise that is what she did do, though. To be honest, I was a bit p… cross with her, like. I was knackered too, but although it ain't far, she might of offered to drop me off at home. But oh no. Off she goes in the car, and I had to walk. Sometimes she was a bit like that. Mikey says she is "entitled", but I think she is just a bit, like, selfish.'

'Perhaps we could have that cup of tea now, Karen,' said DI Francis.

Chapter 24

She sat on the edge of the thin mattress and felt as if her head would explode.

Those pills had given her a stomach upset, and now she had what she imagined would be described as a migraine. She could barely move. Everything hurt.

Maybe this was her punishment. If so, then she deserved it, and worse. Much, much worse.

'Oh, Elliot,' she found herself saying out loud. 'I am so very, very sorry.' And with that, she allowed herself to fall sideways onto the bed and curled into a tight ball as, at last, the blissful unconsciousness of long-awaited sleep overtook her.

***

'I sorry, Doctor Brown, no thinking I can work here no more.'

'Whatever has happened, Lena? Are you all right?' Dr Brown held the telephone a little closer to his ear, the better to catch what she said.

'Yes. All right, yes, but.'

'But what? Has something happened to Andrew?'

'No, but yes. Is best you coming see, Doctor Brown. Best you coming, yes.'

***

Returning from the swirling depths of the deep drug-induced sleep, the sharp knock on the door of the mobile home startled Emma.

Nobody, apart from the contractors and the owners, knew she was here, on this deserted holiday home site out of season, she was sure, and it was very early in the morning.

'Emma?' called a voice she recognised, and she hurried to open the door.

'Panda!'

'Well, you hid yourself away very effectively. I've had the devil's own job tracking you down …'

'Panda, I …'

'Eventually I got the address out of one of your decorators up at the flat, but I'd already been to the hotel you stayed in and missed you there.'

'I'm sorry, I ...'

'The flat looks good. Oh, and by the way, you're fired.'

'What?'

'Well, you can't be surprised. If killing the boss isn't grounds for dismissal, I'm not sure what is.'

Emma wondered whether to invite Panda in. She had not seen her since they were in the hospital, and while she looked considerably better than she did then, her face was bruised, and her once shapely nose was still bandaged and looked slightly crooked.

'Although I had thought of offering you a full partnership so we could run the estate agency together, I decided against it. If we were measuring up a top-floor flat, for example, I would find the urge to push you out of the window almost irresistible. And I should only waste my time in the office looking up how to cut the brake-pipes on your car on the internet.'

'Would you ...'

'I won't come in, thank you. I never feel safe in these caravan things. Such a fire hazard. Did you know they have wooden frames, and what with the naked flames from the gas appliances, you could find that this place burned down around your ears overnight with you in it.'

Emma recoiled at the bitter tone of Panda's voice.

'I assume that we can take your serving notice to quit the flat as read? It was good of you to get it cleaned up to remove my husband's blood, but presumably you have no intention of going back there. I'm having the locks changed tomorrow anyway.'

'I ...'

'Incidentally, I happen to know that it is against the Planning rules to occupy these holiday places out of season. Were anyone to report you for living here, by any chance ...'

'Now look, Panda ...'

'No, you look, Emma. It is time you left here and went away. Far away. Because if I find you, I will enjoy making your life an absolute hell. You needn't worry that I will kill you, as you killed my husband, but you might wish I had, if I catch you.'

Emma started to close the door.

'Run, Emma. Run away. I'll drop by tomorrow to make sure you have gone.'

Chapter 25

'Yes, she called about five minutes ago, sir. I thought I'd go straight over to the holiday park.'

'I'll come with you later on, Curtis,' said DI Francis. 'But first, I think we had better locate and pull in Panda Markham for a chat.'

***

Sir Lemuel could hear the conversation in his mind now:
'Can't stop, Pop, I just need to pick up the boys' new bikes ready for their birthday and nip into the office for something. I'll be back in time for the meeting.'

There was no getting away from it; he was certain she did say she was going to the office. That is what the policemen had been asking about.

His daughter. His only daughter. How had that precious little girl he had loved to distraction turned into this? And Elliot, poor Elliot. He had liked that boy, and he did not deserve what had happened.

Their peaceful life had been so comprehensively upended now, and could never be the same, now that the twins had lost their father.

Was it all his daughter's fault?

Perhaps not.

Shaking his head, Sir Lemuel realised that he knew what he had to do, and he reached for the telephone and began to dial.

**

Just as he was about to leave the consulting rooms to answer Lena's plea, Dr Brown had taken a call from the lawyer.

He explained that Guy Lombardi had received a three-year prison sentence at Court the previous day, and while attempts at recovery continued, some thirty per cent of the money he embezzled from Andrew had so far been identified. The solicitor was able to confidently predict that more was to follow shortly.

At the flat, Dr Brown was shocked by the drawing, but had to admit that he was impressed by it.

The woman's straight upright back, with her hair

flowing and giving the impression of movement, was elegantly drawn. It was in perfect proportion, although the scene beneath her was rather too graphic, as she straddled the man.

Andrew had added a few subtle touches that were not obvious at first glance. The bedding, for example, appeared to be made out of ten-pound notes, and the curtains appeared printed with shadowy coins.

What struck him most, though, was that the woman, Panda Markham, Andrew explained, was holding something, a hammer perhaps, in one raised hand. It was almost hidden in shadow, on the side furthest away from the observer, where she was engaged with her lover. This was the first depiction of anything violent or weapons in any of Andrew's paintings or sketches.

He asked the boy what it meant, but received no sensible answer.

Fortunately, he managed to talk Lena into staying, and they spent the rest of the afternoon explaining to Andrew why images of this type were not appropriate.

***

The effects of the drug had not worn off as Emma

turned off her mobile phone. She felt groggy and heavy.

Had what she had just experienced actually happened. Had Panda really been there?

She closed her eyes briefly, but started to visualise the blood again, so sat down and shook her head.

She wished things had been different. She was very fond of Elliot, and in different circumstances she might even have loved him. But elegant and sophisticated Panda filled his life, and she could never compete with that, even if she had wanted to.

She missed Peter. He was kind and polite, and a considerate lover. On recent evidence that set him apart from Elliot and his violent attack on Panda.

She could not get past that attack. Every thought seemed to lead back to it.

Perhaps she was losing her grip on her sanity. She felt bile and despair rising in her throat.

Chapter 26

Two uniformed officers delivered Panda to the police station.

After leaving the mobile home site, she had returned to her brother's house and was watching the breakfast show on the television when they called.

DI Francis started the interview as soon as she arrived.

'I think you let yourself into the beach hut with the key and somehow tempted Stanley Gurney to join you in there. How did you do that, Mrs Markham? Did you offer him sex?' said DI Francis.

There was a knock at the door, and DS Curtis got up to admit a round, sweating man, who introduced himself as Panda's solicitor. Once he was settled, the interview resumed.

'I suggest you took the beach hut keys back to the office after you had murdered Stanley Gurney in the beach hut called 'Manilla',' said DS Curtis. 'Why did he meet you there, Panda? Before Guy Lombardi incriminated himself, you thought Stanley Gurney was the blackmailer, didn't you? Did you arrange to meet him there and have it out with him, or had you turned the tables on him and threatened to hurt his son Andrew in some way?'

There was another knock on the interview room door, and again DS Curtis got up to answer it.

'Or, did Andrew tell his father that he thought you were involved in stealing his money?' continued DI Francis. 'Did *Stanley* arrange the meeting to confront you with that?'

DS Curtis opened the envelope he had been handed by the policeman outside the door and smiled.

'Which was it, Panda?' said DS Curtis. 'I'm interested, although it doesn't actually matter which version is the truth now, because I've just got this ...'

'Is that what I think it is?' asked DI Francis.

'Yes, sir. The results of the DNA testing. The minute traces of blood on the 'iklwa' belonged to Stanley Gurney, as did the traces of washed-out blood on your tee-shirt, Mrs. Markham, and the little piece of animal skin binding we found in your jeans pocket with the sellotape matched the handle of the 'iklwa' you took from the farmhouse early in the morning on your first visit there, when nobody except the postman saw you.'

DI Frances read through the DNA results while DS Curtis was speaking, and now he nodded.

'Carry on, Detective Sergeant,' he said.

DS Curtis got to his feet.

'Amanda Jane Markham, I'm arresting you for the murder of Stanley Gurney. You do not have to say anything, but ...'

***

Emma tightened the laces on her running shoes and pulled the velcro fastening on the 'Armpocket' mobile phone holder off her upper arm and threw it on the bed. She had tried several times, but had not managed to get the blood stains off it, and now she did not want it there as a reminder of what had happened. Other than that, her preparations were purely mechanical, and she went through the motions, the same as every other morning.

Earlier, she had called the police about Panda's visit, but could not clear her mind or shake off the vision of Elliot's blood. However, it was time for her morning run, and although she was upset and it was drizzling, even in normal times, she never felt right if she missed that.

She had begun to think that she would never be released from the pain and the thoughts which went round and round in her head. She didn't expect the run to help much in itself, but it was the only part of her routine left, and the more she thought about it, the more she realised that she could use it as an escape, at last, from this tumultuous waking nightmare.

She ran as hard as she could, as soon as she was out of the caravan, oblivious to the tears coursing down her face, the splitting pain in her head, and the fine rain beginning to soak the cliff path she knew so well, where she ran every day.

***

As soon as he saw her from his boat, just off shore, Errol grabbed his mobile phone and dialled 999.

He said she appeared to be running in the air as she came over the edge of the cliff, thirty metres up.

'I seen that woman running along the cliff edge before. Same time every day, come rain or shine, reg'lar as clockwork. You could set your watch by her. You wouldn't get me up there, though. Dangerous that path is.'

He had not seen the end of her fall, but he knew.

Chapter 27

Six months later.

They sat down at the dining table, and Susie cleared a space amongst all the baby clutter for the paperwork.

'So, what was it like, then?'

'Well, I've got to say it was pretty much ideal, but it is a long way away, and from that point of view it is not what I'd originally envisioned.'

'But you liked it?'

'Quite honestly, Susie, I loved it. I'll show you all the figures in a minute, but the most important thing is whether we, you, I mean, fancy moving away from here and starting afresh down there. How would you really feel about it?'

Susie readjusted the sleeping baby in her arms and looked at her husband. He was grinning from ear to ear, like an excited schoolboy.

'There is a lot to think about. I'd have to look into schools and all that sort of thing, but I know you have wanted to set up on your own for so long, and I think the time is right, now.'

'I have Susie, and as you know, I've been looking around for the right sort of thing for ages. I just hadn't expected it to turn up quite so far away.'

'Let's have a look at the details then, Simon. What did you say it was called?'

'Elliots. I've found out that was his first name … the owner chappy, who has died, which is why it is up for sale. That gave me an idea, Susie, maybe we could rename it after Dicky!'

'His name is Richard, Simon. I wish you wouldn't keep calling him Dicky.'

'No. Yes. That's what I mean, old girl. We could rebrand it as Richard's Estate Agency!'

'Oh, Simon. That's lovely!'

***

Mikey sat with his coffee behind the closed window blinds, surrounded by his buckets and window cleaning paraphernalia.

'I'm gonna have to put them up to do the inside,

babe. That be alright?'

'I 'spose so. Gotta be done, ain't it, even though we ain't open for business. Sir Lemuel says I gotta keep everything clean and nice, like, while it's up for sale. That's why 'e is still paying me.'

Karen got up to take her empty cup to the little kitchen.

'So, what was 'e like, this bloke what come?'

'He was nice. Posh, like, and quite old. Well, maybe not that old, but 'e 'ad grey hair and that.'

'Do you think 'e would keep you on, if 'e was interested in buying it?'

'I dunno. He was nice, I mean perlite, like, but it was 'ard to say what he was thinking. Mind you, 'e did 'ave a broad grin on 'is face when 'e left.'

Mikey had joined her in the kitchen and caressed her bottom.

'Probably been looking at you, babe. You always 'ave that effect on me, if you know what I mean.'

'Shut up, Mikey! And get your hands off, you great mutt!'

'Why? Nobody is gonna come in, are they?'

'You never know. Sir Lemuel's Land Rover is in the

car park at the back, so 'e must be in the town. Maybe he will call in 'ere, like!'

***

It had been over five years since Emma left King and Rutter, said goodbye to Simon Hamilton-Smythe, and moved down to the little coastal town to start a new life.

Simon would not even have glanced at the advertisement in the 'businesses for sale' section of 'The Negotiator' magazine when it arrived, had it not been for the fact that he recognised the name of the little town she had taken herself off to.

He scanned the adverts halfheartedly every month as he hung onto his dream of one day setting up in business on his own, but with a new baby and a substantial mortgage to cope with, such plans seemed remote.

He had progressed steadily through the ranks at King and Rutter since splitting up with Emma, and was now in charge of six of the firm's fifteen branch offices. He had been responsible for finding and opening two of those branches, so he knew what was involved in setting them up, as well as how to evaluate all the costs. He also knew how to prepare a 'business case' to present to his employers and the banks that funded them. But finding the right opportunity to put his experience into practice on his own account had so far eluded him, and he was very much aware of the risks.

Since he met and married Susie three years ago, he had shared his dream with her, and she had been encouraging initially. But the arrival of little Dicky had inevitably changed everything and put Simon's dream on the back burner.

Susie had left her secure and quite senior job at the local council, and before the statutory paid maternity leave came to an end, she had announced that she would not be returning to her job and intended to be a stay-at-home mum. That news caused their first row, but it soon blew over when Simon held little Dicky in his arms and came to realise just how precious parenting time was.

Maybe Susie could do the accounts or something from home, if he did buy a business of his own, he thought.

***

Stanley Gurney's cottage had been sold to some out-of-town people to be used as a holiday home.

Sir Lemuel Fulton-Marks was not delighted about that, but it would have to do. He would much rather see it let to another fishing family, but when Andrew sold the crabbing licence and the boat he had inherited to the Richards family, that idea became unlikely.

Much of his time had been taken up with the complicated and long-winded business of setting up a 'Trust' for Panda and Elliot's twin sons, with the family solicitor. Sir Lemuel, as principal trustee and administrator, had much to do, and just getting the various properties involved sorted out took time.

Elliot owned the estate agent's office premises outright and had recently signed a long-term lease on an empty shop in the rather exclusive town, just up the coast, where he proposed to open a new branch. The matter was complicated because the business had not yet taken possession of the shop, and it would need some modernisation and building works to separate it from the upmarket fine-art auctioneers' business next door, which it originally formed part of.

Then there was the matter of the house where Elliot and Panda had lived. That was also owned outright, without a mortgage to complicate matters, but it was a valuable asset which represented the main part of the twins' inheritance. Sir Lemuel was in the process of having it cleared and redecorated in preparation to rent it out for the time being. The boys would continue to live with his son, Panda's brother, although with Panda in prison, it was not clear what their long-term future, or that of the house, would be.

Then there were the various properties Elliot had inherited or gathered up over the years. Two small houses and four concrete holiday bungalows were leased out, and there was the empty flat, which Elliot had bought at some point in an auction. But most complicated and frustrating was the semi-derelict terraced house in France, which Elliot's father had acquired as a holiday home many years ago. It was now in need of major structural repairs, and part of the roof had fallen in.

The French lawyer they got involved said it was actually fortunate that the roof had collapsed, rendering the building uninhabitable, because it removed the threat of squatters taking it over. But it had little value in its present state, and having declared that it was a dangerous structure, the French authorities wanted something done. Elliot, it emerged, had dodged the issue for several years, and now there was some pressure to sort it out.

As he finished his call with the lawyer, paid his bill at the coffee shop and strolled back over the road to his Land Rover, the heavy padlock he had just purchased bumped in his pocket. At least when he got back to the house, he could walk down the garden and make sure that the gate leading to the narrow cliff path at the bottom was securely locked up. That would add to the measures he planned to take to make sure squatters could not get into Elliot and Panda's former home before he could let it out.

Chapter 28

Susie and Simon had fixed up a second viewing of the estate agency, this time together.

Susie had never been to the little seaside town before and was a little apprehensive, but she looked again at the photographs on his phone that Simon had taken, as she sat in the back of the car. They had to get used to the front seat being occupied by the baby's backwards-facing car seat, and she had spent the last few miles waving and making gurgling sounds at her happy baby.

'The pipeline is quite strong, actually,' Simon was saying. 'There are several sales still going through, although the office is currently shut, and when I asked around, it seems the business has a good reputation locally. There is also a small but solid rental management income stream, although most of the properties seem to be owned by this Fulton-Marks character, who heads up the trust that is selling the business. I guess it would be wise to keep in with him.'

'Isn't that who we are supposed to be meeting there,

Simon?'

'Yes, although last time I was met by this busty young girl who unlocked the door dressed in jeans and trainers. Not what I was expecting at all.'

'You prefer them flat-chested?'

'No!' laughed Simon. 'I mean, she wasn't dressed like an estate agent, although she said she worked there. I think she is an office junior or something.'

'Are there any other staff?'

'Not now. I haven't got to the bottom of that, but the accounts show payments to a senior negotiator who must have been quite good, judging by the amount of commission she was raking in.'

'It looks quite profitable, though.'

'Yes, very much so. Although did you notice that huge postal bill in the breakdown? Some of the things they do are a bit old-fashioned. That girl … Karen, I think it was, said they still do big mail-outs of printed details to all their applicants. That will be the first thing I'll stop, if we go ahead with this. It will save a small fortune.'

'Got it all worked out, haven't you?'

'I've got to be honest, old girl, I've looked at several businesses like this when they come up for sale over the years, but this is the first time I've ever felt really comfortable about one. Something about this is very attractive.'

'Are you sure it is not just the busty office junior you are finding attractive?'

***

As he raised the blinds, Sir Lemuel Fulton-Marks made sure Karen knew what to do.

'So they will have driven quite a long way, and I'd like you to offer them tea and coffee when they arrive, please. Are there any biscuits available?'

'Biscuits? Nah … I mean no sir, we ain't got none.'

'Well, would you mind popping along to the shops and buying a tin of biscuits, please, Karen, and make sure there is enough coffee and so on.'

Sir Lemuel reached into his pocket and pulled out a twenty-pound note.

'And can you get some polish and give these desks a do, while you are at it. We want everything to look at its best.'

'Right-ho,' said Karen. 'An' I'm sorry I ain't got dressed up, like. I realise I shouldn't of wore me jeans to the office, sir. Won't happen again.'

'Don't worry about that, Karen. I'm sure they won't be looking at you,' said Sir Lemuel, although he quite enjoyed surreptitiously looking at her himself, as she flicked a duster about and tidied up.

***

DS Curtis closed down the file on his computer. His report on Emma Johnson's death was all typed up and ready to be filed away.

It was a pity that things turned out as they did, and this morning, as he drove past the estate agent's office, he remembered again how distraught poor little Karen was when she was told about Emma's suicide. She was a good kid, that one, and he wondered what would happen to her.

Presumably, the estate agent business would close down, and that would be her out of a job. It was tough for these youngsters to get a job around here as it was, and those without much by way of formal education particularly struggled. She came from a decent enough family, at least, and unlike some on the estate where she lived, had kept herself out of trouble.

Perhaps she will leave the area, he thought. Many did and often ended up in London, and who knows what fate. Karen was the sort of girl who might attract some attention, maybe the wrong sort of attention, and he hoped she would be all right.

Chapter 29

'I expect property prices around here are somewhat cheaper than in your area,' said Sir Lemuel, conversationally. 'Where was it again?'

'Surrey, London borders,' replied Simon. 'I'm sure you are right.'

Simon was studying the paperwork as he sat in one of the client chairs in the front office.

'I think your son has certainly made a hit with young Karen,' Sir Lemuel observed, as the giggles and gurgling noises in the back office continued.

Karen was entranced with the baby, and having shyly asked if she could hold him, was now delighted to be entertaining him. No matter that he had been sick on her top and on her jeans, it would wash out, she was sure.

Susie was also enjoying a few precious moments of rest without having to attend to the baby and was happy to sit in one of the customer's chairs, watching Karen play with the child.

'What is the rental market like around here?' asked Simon. 'We shall need to sell our house, and we will have to rent something down here while that is going through, if we do this.'

'I'm sorry,' said Sir Lemuel. 'You see, I'm not really involved in this business, and I don't feel qualified to give an opinion on that. What I can tell you, though, is that Elliot, my son-in-law, owned a flat over the road, which is currently empty and has just been redecorated. If it would help you, I suppose there is no reason why you could not use that for a while, at least until you get settled.'

'Well, that is something to think about, yes,' said Susie. 'Could we see it while we are here?'

Simon smiled as he realised Susie was getting keen on the idea.

'I see no reason why not,' said Sir Lemuel. 'If you like, we could go round it on our way back from looking at the new premises further up the coast. By the way, I did say you don't have to take the empty shop if you don't want to, didn't I?'

'Yes, and that would be great, Sir Lemuel. Thank you. But you will have to squash in the back of our car, if you don't mind, because of the baby seat.'

'Can I come?' said Karen.

***

In a way, it was a little bit of a holiday, Dr Brown told Lena, on his return to London.

Overseeing the clearing out of Stanley Gurney's cottage was not really hard work; the contractors did all the heavy lifting, but given that Dr Brown rarely bothered to take holidays, it did make something of a change for him.

'The sea air will do good, too,' offered Lena.

Of course, Andrew could not be persuaded to join in and showed no interest in saying goodbye to his family home. All he said on the matter was that any of his paintings left in the cottage could be sold, for all he cared.

He actually seemed quite relieved when his father's boat was sold, and Dr Brown was interested in his reaction to this news. He would not be drawn on why, but Lena suggested that perhaps the boat represented his intense fear of the sea, which may account for it.

Planning for Andrew's future was no less difficult now, despite the recovery of a substantial amount of the money Guy Lombardi stole from him. Whilst he may be financially secure, his needs were such that he could not live independently, and while the burden of paying Lena's wages was now removed from Dr Brown, Andrew was a grown man with a long life ahead of him, and he would probably outlive Lena and Dr Brown by many years.

The situation had been considerably improved by the sale of three more of the intricate and masterful paintings Andrew produced, and it was interesting and somewhat encouraging from a financial point of view that once a picture was finished, Andrew lost interest in it and was quite content to see his work sold. But there was a new trend developing in his work.

Andrew became frustrated initially by his perceived inability to paint people. He complained that, try as he might, he could not capture the essence, or as he put it, the 'life' of a person on canvas.

He had asked both Lena and Dr Brown to sit for him as he sketched them, and had tried to work from photographs. But he was disappointed with the results and, with only a handful of exceptions, immediately destroyed his work.

Lena delivered his request for a full-length mirror on wheels to be purchased, when his attempts at a self-portrait were frustrated by the fixed mirrors in the flat, which he could not move to capture the light as he wanted it. And when it was provided, he sat for hours staring at his reflection with his sketch pad on his lap.

There was trouble when Lena was awoken in the middle of the night by a crash, and discovered Andrew had smashed the mirror in frustration and cut himself with one of the shards of glass.

'I cannot say for sure, but maybe he cut himself with the glass on purpose,' Lena whispered to Dr Brown, as Andrew refused to leave his bed the next morning.

***

Sir Lemuel was quite content to give Simon and Susie 'first refusal' for a fortnight to enable them to complete their appraisal and secure the loan they would need from a bank.

In truth, there had been no other interest in the sale of the estate agency business and only one viewing, so Sir Lemuel was not taking any risks.

It was to be the busiest fortnight of Simon's life, and the relaxing time with his new family he described to his employer when he put in his holiday request was not entirely truthful.

Simon sat up long into the night, refining his cash-flow forecasts and adding market research details and staffing predictions to his business plan, as he gathered them.

He visited the little seaside town and the nearby

town where the empty shop stood several times, and decided, after much heart searching, that he would need to concentrate on the original business for a while before he could think about expanding into a second premises. He was relieved that Sir Lemuel was happy to exclude the empty shop from the deal, especially when he said that he would hold onto the premises for the time being and look for another use or perhaps delay completion on the lease transfer if he could. Maybe Simon would like to reopen negotiations on that at some point in the future, if it was still in his control, Sir Lemuel offered.

In truth, Sir Lemuel needed to get a deal done and felt that he should secure a buyer before the existing business in the functioning agency melted away. He also felt a duty to try to secure employment for young Karen with the new owners, and he could not continue to pay her just to be a caretaker of the premises forever.

Simon was going to need staff, and agreed that he would take Karen on if they could agree on terms.

They had also been quietly doing their homework on the competition in the surrounding towns.

Simon had asked Susie to go into some of the local agents and arrange to view a couple of properties with specific negotiators he had picked out. He then met them at the properties, and if they performed well, he put them on his shortlist. On the third attempt, he struck gold in the form of a bright young man named Gary Kirby, and he offered him a job on the spot.

Meanwhile, Susie kept notes on each of the receptionists and other staff she met while Simon waited in the car with the baby, and she created a shortlist for him to consider for an office-based post, if one could be persuaded to leave their current employers.

It was a tactic that would be considered a little underhanded by his competitors and cause some temporary friction, he was sure, but he had employed it several times in the past for King and Rutter when they expanded, and it worked well. He could take the flak if he got the best staff with the local knowledge he needed.

Back home, Simon arranged a confidential meeting with the manager of the bank King and Rutter used, whom he had carefully cultivated over the years, and presented his business plan. As a result of that encouraging meeting, he made an offer for the Elliots' estate agency and asked if the vacant flat could be let to them for six months rent-free as part of the deal.

As in any negotiation, there was a little bit of give and take. Finally, a three-month rent-free period was agreed for the flat, and a price for the freehold of the estate agency business, furniture, fittings and 'goodwill' was agreed.

On his first day back at work after his so-called holiday, Simon went to see his boss, handed in his resignation and put his house on the market.

This was it. He was going for it at last. He was on his way, and he couldn't be happier.

Chapter 30

'It is all very white and a bit soulless, but it will do,' said Simon after his first night in the flat over the road from his new business.

'Well, that's not surprising after what happened in there, like,' said Karen.

'What do you mean?' asked Simon.

Karen blushed bright red. She should not have said that; she should have kept quiet. But before she had to answer, Susie flounced in from the back kitchen, with little Dicky tucked into her arm, attempting to scream the place down.

'Oh! Bless 'im! Can I take 'im?' she enquired.

'With pleasure,' said Susie, handing the bawling baby over.

***

Karen was sitting on the wall looking down over the promenade with her chips as the sun set.

'Well, she's nice, that Susie, 'an the baby's lovely. Adorable little mite 'e is.'

'But 'e embarrassed you, you said?' asked Mikey. 'Askin' awkward questions, like?'

'It was my own fault. I think I got away with it, but I hope 'e don't remember and ask me any more questions, like. Its obvious 'e don't know about Emma or Elliot.'

'I wouldn't worry 'bout it, babe. Bet 'e's forgotten all about it, too.'

'Well, you never worry 'bout anything, do you, Mikey. You don't have to be there all the time, do ya?'

'Y'know, if anyone gives you any trouble, babe, I'll sort 'em out.'

'Shut up, Mikey, it's not like that, an' you know it.'

'Yeah, but … well, I just love you, don't I.'

'Oh, Mikey, you big softy!'

Karen threw her arms around him.

'Look out! You'll drop your chips!' said Mikey.

***

It wasn't quite six-fifteen when Simon quietly closed

the front door and let himself out of the building.

The baby had been restless most of the night, and the flat was chilly, so Susie had taken him into their bed, and finally they had both drifted off to sleep. But by then Simon was wide awake, and determined not to disturb them, he left a note, and decided to go and look at his new office. He had given himself three weeks to get it all ready before Garry Kirby joined the business in time for the re-opening, and he wanted to plan what needed to be done.

The short walk down the hill and around the corner freshened him up, and the sun was beginning to warm the spring morning.

Simon looked around him at the little town as he strolled past the recreation ground, with its brightly coloured nodding daffodils in the trim flower borders by the solid-looking brick bus shelter. Whilst the grass on the playing fields was green and flat here, approaching from this angle, the road sloped quite steeply down towards the sea, which hung on the horizon like a quiet haze in the distance.

In front of him and down to the left, the church, with its square steeple and Gothic arches, gave a sense of permanence to the landscape. The shops, such as they were at this end of the town, straggled in two and three-storey lines stepping down to the cliffs, just around the bend.

His own newly acquired piece of this town was on a corner, at the end of a short terrace built on three levels. As the former Victorian grocer's shop, which now formed the estate agent's office, came into view, he could see lights in one of the windows of the two flats, long since sold off on long leaseholds, above it.

He had not taken much notice of these flats before, in all the excitement, except to note from the deeds that they shared some of the spaces in the carpark at the rear, accessed off a side road. He now owned five parking spaces in this area, one of which was covered by a rickety corrugated iron garage, under a patched and wavy pitched roof with grass growing in the gutter, which had clearly seen better days. So far, he had only been able to glance into this structure, which, behind its rotting timber doors, concealed all the paraphernalia needed to manage the 'for sale' boards the business used.

Amongst the clutter there were boxes of nails and screws on dusty, leaning shelves, and tools ranging from a sledgehammer and a set of garden shears, to screw drivers and an electric drill. Many generations of the agent's boards and advertising hoardings in various states of disrepair leaned against the walls amongst timber posts, and scattered on the floor, painted signs reading 'sold' or 'under offer', waited to be attached to the signs as appropriate.

Simon had noticed that, unlike the plastic and

printed signs King and Rutter used, all these items were sign-written, presumably by some local artisan. The sign over the shop front window was the same, not the usual internally lit box arrangement which graced most modern premises. Simon made a mental note to find the local plastic sign maker and get a price for the re-branded 'Richards' signs he intended to replace all that old-fashioned stuff with.

Now at the door, he read the gold lettering on the glass, which proclaimed the office hours the business kept and the telephone and Fax numbers they used.

Fax number? Simon smiled to himself. It was so old-school. All that would have to be replaced with the website and email address in due course. And looking up, there was the big painted sign over the window with its pale blue background and white lettering picked out by black edging, as replicated on the agent's signs and printed details. As far as he could see, the sign wasn't even illuminated.

It would all have to go, of course.

Chapter 31

DI Francis called DS Curtis over for a chat.

'I've heard from our friendly postman, Jim Pike, this morning.'

'Who?'

'The postman. You know, the one who gave evidence against Panda Markham when he gave her the post on Sir Lemuel's driveway.'

'Oh, him. What did he want?'

'I'm not sure how much store I put by this, to be honest, but he said he stops for a drink after work sometimes and sees Errol Richards in the bar sometimes. Errol is expressing doubts about whether Emma Johnson actually committed suicide.'

'I've just finished the paperwork on all that.'

'Yes, well. Would you mind dropping in on Errol, perhaps not in front of his family, given their reputation, and see if this is just pub banter.'

'Really? Do you think there was anything to suggest that it wasn't suicide?'

'No, I don't, Detective Sergeant, but then I was not an eyewitness to the incident, and Errol was.'

'Right,' sighed DS Curtis. 'I'll see if I can find Errol, shall I?'

'Yes, please.'

***

'See, 'e's brung in a new computer system an' I've got to 'elp 'im put all the stuff on there. There is a big new photocopier thing coming too. I seen a picture. Gawd knows 'ow it works.'

'But why do you have to stay on late?'

'We got to do it all in one go, 'e says, and this new bloke, Gary something, is coming in tomorrow to see it.'

'That's a bummer.'

'I know, Mikey. But I will get extra money, 'e says, if I stay and help 'im to understand the filing system, and put the applicants names … that's, like, what they call the buyers, on it, an' that.'

'Well, I 'spose you'll 'ave to. On a Friday night, an' all!'

'I gotta go, 'e is coming back. Laters.'

***

Simon was excited. Earlier, the new computer system had been delivered and set up, and the monitor on his desk was sitting with an icon blinking at him and the words 'add data?' scrolling across the bottom of the screen.

It was the latest version of the same system King and Rutter had installed in London, and it integrated seamlessly with the new digital printer, which was capable, amongst other things, of producing 'professional quality' brochures on thick card and even binding the pages together like a book.

In 'desktop publishing' mode, it could produce full colour property particulars rapidly and even print off photos to put in the window. It could also link to the new seventy-inch TV screen, which was due to be delivered soon, to display pictures and details in the window.

In a couple of weeks, the new camera and drone system would arrive, and they would receive training on how to create overhead 'fly-by' footage of the houses they had for sale, to go up on the website and be projected on the big screen. None of the local competitors had that. None of them!

Simon couldn't wait.

***

'So I wondered, Simon, if you would like to accompany me to the Cricket Club tomorrow evening,' said Sir Lemuel. 'It is the first game of the season, and there are several people there, that is to say, local solicitors and whatnot, who you might like to meet. But more important than that, we need to discuss the sponsorship arrangements. Elliots provided some sponsorship in return for advertising for many years, and of course, we would like to continue the arrangement if we could.'

'I must confess I hadn't considered anything like that,' said Simon. 'Are you on the committee there?'

'I'm the President, as it happens. The other folk you may meet could get you into the golf club, possibly. I'm sure that would be handy. Shall I meet you there? Shall we say four o'clock tomorrow?'

***

'So, can you explain to me how the applicant information is filed, Karen?'

'Sure, it's easy. Emma come up with this system, and even Elliot understood it.'

'I'm sorry? Did you say Emma?'

'Erm, yeah.'

'Did she work here recently?'

'Well, yeah, until …'

'Was that Emma Johnson by any chance?'

'Yes.'

'Crikey, so she was still here after all these years!'

'I'm sorry, I don't think I understand, Simon?'

'Emma, Emma Johnson. I used to work with her years ago, assuming it is the same one. I knew she moved down here, but I didn't know exactly where she worked. Do you know where she went, Karen? How long ago did she leave?'

Karen rummaged in the desk for the tissue box.

'Karen? What's wrong? Are you … are you crying?'

***

'I'm terribly sorry, Simon, I should have told you before, and it shouldn't have fallen on Karen to have to explain it all to you.' Sir Lemuel held the phone away from his face and blew his nose. 'It is all so very sad.'

'I'm not sure what to say,' said Simon. 'This has come as a shock.'

'Yes, I daresay. Look, could we talk it through when we meet tomorrow at the Cricket Club? I'm not sure how much Karen has said, but if it is upsetting her, please apologise on my behalf. And … and might it be better to let her go home now, given the circumstances? It is nearly half past six, after all.'

Chapter 32

DS Curtis approached the bar.

'Can I have a quiet word, Errol?'

'Oh, bladdy hell! You!' spluttered Errol into his beer. 'I ain't done nuffin … what d'yer want?'

'Just a quiet word … shall we sit over here?' DS Curtis indicated an uncomfortable-looking wooden bench in a quiet corner by the window.

As they settled on the seat, Errol looked even more uncomfortable than the policeman felt.

'So, nothing to be alarmed about, Errol, it is just that I understand you might have information regarding Emma Johnson's death, which you witnessed from your boat.'

'I already made a statement about that …'

'I know, Errol, I just wondered if, on reflection, you still considered it to be suicide?'

'Who you been talking to? I didn't say that.'

'Well, my sources say you have been casting doubts and suggesting it might have been murder. What made you think that, Errol?'

'Well, I ain't … I mean … I was offshore, wasn't I … I couldn't exactly see that well, at that distance.'

'But you agreed with the officer you spoke to at the time that she appeared to run off the top of the cliff?'

'Well, what I said was it looked like she was running when she was in the air.'

'Running out from the cliff. Yes, that is what it was, wasn't it?'

'No. Not from the cliff … running towards the cliff … in the air …like she was trying to run back onto it again.'

'But …'

'An' that ain't all, although I'm really not so certain about this … see the boat was heaving up and down where I was stood, off the shore, 'cos the tide was on the turn. One minute I could see the top of the cliff, and the next not. I told that woman policeman that.'

'What does that mean …'

'Well, the bit I ain't sure about at all is when the boat rose up, after she came over, see, I thought I might have glimpsed the gate, you know, in the tall wall up there. I thought it was closing. But I've thought about this, and I really couldn't swear to it. I thought maybe she had come through that gate, but when I thought about it after, I never seen her coming through there. She always ran along the path past there, from the town, like. Reg'lar as clockwork she was, every day. Rain or shine.'

'So you think someone was going through the gate?'

'I didn't see no-one, I just saw, or thought I saw, the gate closing'

'Go on.'

'Well, that got me thinking. What if someone had come out of the gate and bumped into her ... it is very narrow up there ... and maybe pushed her. An' if that happened per'aps it weren't an accident ...'

'I see,'

'Well, you gotta admit it could 'appen, couldn't it?'

'But you saw nobody, and you are not sure that you actually did see the gate moving at all?'

'Well, told yer, didn't I. I was riding the swell. Only caught a glimpse for a split second as she fell.'

'Or was pushed.'

'Or was pushed, as you say.'

'How long have you been in here this afternoon, Errol?'

'A while. Why?'

'And how much have you had to drink?'

'I ain't pissed, if that's what you are thinking. I can't afford to drink fast, so I makes it last before I has to go home for me tea. I've only had … what … four.'

'Why don't you go straight home when you finish and get cleaned up before you come out?'

DS Curtis was finding the odiferous mix of fish, beer and sweat was closing up his sinuses.

'Dunno. Well, yes, I do know. You've met my mum ain'tcha?'

'Yes.'

'Well, there you are then. Speaking of which, I'd better get home or …'

'OK, Errol, thanks for talking to me. But can I ask you to keep what you just told me to yourself now, please? I may need to talk to you about it again.'

***

'Ah, there you are, Simon,' Sir Lemuel said. 'Glad you could come. Perhaps we could have a chat in the clubhouse before I introduce you to the folks here. I'd like to clear the air.'

Simon was ushered into a side room at the back of the building with an oversized table filling most of the available space.

'Look, I'm frightfully sorry about all this coming out as it did. Is little Karen OK?'

'Yes, I sent her home after our telephone conversation, as you suggested, and she seemed fine this morning.'

'You had her working again this morning? On a Saturday?'

'Well, yes. We had to finish what we started yesterday, and I wanted her to meet the new negotiator who came in to see our new systems.'

'I see. Well, needs must, I suppose, but don't forget she is only seventeen …'

'Don't worry, I'll make sure she is all right.'

'I'm sure you will. Now then …'

'Yes. Perhaps we had better start from the beginning. I have not mentioned any of this to my wife yet, and if I told her what happened in the flat you rented to us, I think she would go straight back to London. I don't think we would have taken it, had we known, but now we are stuck. Can you please tell me what exactly happened to Emma?

'Once again, Simon, I really am desperately sorry about this, but I have come up with something which may go some way to making it up to you.'

'Yes, well. I'd really like to know about Emma, Sir Lemuel, if you don't mind. I knew her, you know, and several years ago we were … close.'

'Of course. I see. Well, it really was the most frightful series of events that led to the accident and then to her … to her death. You see what happened is this …'

Chapter 33

'And the doctor said the cut on his arm seemed to be accidental, Lena? No suspicion of self-harming, was there?'

'No, is all good, Dr Brown. Andrew needed the five stitch but was not very serious deep cut. Not that you would think from the way he squeal when he stitched up. I'm thinking maybe the neighbours frightened is murder going on!'

'Oh dear. I'm only sorry I was away at this conference, and I wasn't there to support you. But I'll be back this evening, and I'll come straight round to see you both.'

'Is good. The Andrew will calm down more when he sees you. But don't worry for me, I seen much worse. One of my previous patients was always cutting her wrists. Blood all over. I know the signs and is nothing like that. He just frustrated not do the drawing so good. Maybe he give up on the people painting now, who knows.'

'That is the thing about Andrew, Lena. He is a most

unusual case, that doesn't seem to follow the more expected patterns. He is constantly surprising me, which is what makes him so interesting.'

'Maybe one day you write a book, Dr Brown!'

'Actually, Lena, I already am ...'

'Oh! Am I in it?'

'Of course, and if, and when, it gets published, you will see that it gives you a glowing reference, as well as my deepest thanks and respect.'

***

Simon was very tired, and perhaps that contributed to it, but now that he was on his own, he felt like crying. He had not gone home after his meeting at the cricket club, and went, instead, to the office, where he was sitting alone in the dark.

Obviously, he had never told Susie about how he felt about Emma, but the scars were still there.

It was not that the two women ever met, or that Susie was a particularly jealous type, but when Emma dumped Simon and moved away, it took him a long time to get over her, if he ever had. Susie knew he had a serious relationship in the past, but he had never been able to tell her, or anyone else, how hurt he was by the experience.

Simon had read once that almost everyone has one great romance in their life that lives with them long after it is over, deep inside, and is never forgotten. He identified with that immediately, and Emma was always there, on the edges of his consciousness, although when he met and married Susie, he had tried hard to finally put her out of his mind.

Now, as he sat alone amongst the empty computer boxes and tried to deal with the horrible events Sir Lemuel Fulton-Marks had explained to him, the feelings he had been holding back for Emma for years all rushed into his mind again, and with his elbows on the desk, he put his head in his hands as the sobs became uncontrollable, and wracked his body.

***

Mikey should have been playing cricket this afternoon. It was the first match of the new season, after all. But he had told the team captain that he was unavailable, so that he could spend time with Karen and offer her some comfort.

'You feelin' alright now, babe?' he asked.

'Yeah, I'm much better now, ta. Tea an' a cuddle will

soon pick anyone up, and these scones are lovely.'

'My mum always said this was the best tea shop in town, an' only the best will do fer my girl.'

'You big lump, Mikey.'

'That's me, babe. Soft as s... butter, I am.'

'I'm sorry you missed your cricket. Is it on again next week? I could come an' help with the teas if you like.'

'That would be great. They are a bit worried about losing sponsors this year, what with Elliot ... I mean, now things are changing. But we have a much better team now, an' we could even move up the table a bit if ...'

'Mikey ...'

'Yes, babe?'

'If you've finished your tea, I wouldn't half mind that cuddle now.'

Chapter 34

DS Curtis sat in front of DI Francis's desk and waited for him to return from the coffee machine.

'So what do you think?' said DI Francis, placing his coffee on an old beermat.

'Initially, I thought he could be just embellishing what he saw to impress his pub mates. He is not the brightest bulb in the chandelier, after all. But then, the more I listened to him, the more I started to believe that perhaps he had seen more than he said to start with. The problem with this is that even if he is right, he is the only witness we have. Nobody else was about at that time in the morning, unsurprisingly.'

'He said that Emma Johnson always took her run at the same time each morning, and that you could set your watch by her. Might there be any other joggers or delivery people, or even other fishermen who knew her routine, do you think?'

'Not that we have discovered so far.'

'She had a boyfriend, didn't she?'

'Yes, we got his name from the yoga class she attended. Peter something. He works for HM Customs and Excise up in town, I think.'

'Did he jog?'

'I don't think so, and Emma ran, rather than jogged.'

'I'm not sure what the difference is,' said DI Francis, smiling. 'Never been into all that healthy stuff, myself.'

'No, sir,' said DS Curtis, trying not to look at his superior officer's spreading belly, pushed up against the desk.

'Well, it wouldn't do any harm to have another chat with the boyfriend, I suppose. He might know the route she took each day, at least.'

'The gate Errol referred to is in the tall wall at the bottom of Elliot and Panda Markham's garden. We know they employed a gardener. I could check who that is if you like.'

'Yes, better do that. He is the only other person I can think of who might need access to their garden. Maybe he starts work that early in the morning ... perhaps ...'

'I'll check it out, sir.' DS Curtis got up from his chair

and went in search of WPC Linda Pope. She knew most of the tradesmen in the town and might know who this gardener was.

***

Their meeting on Saturday morning was useful, and it must be said, Gary Kirby was impressed with the new computer system and the plans Simon had for the business. But there were still unresolved issues to deal with before Gary would commit to joining the company, so a further meeting had been arranged for this evening.

With the blinds drawn on the office windows, Simon showed the young man through to the more comfortable room at the rear of the premises, previously used as Elliot's office.

At twenty five years old, Gary was still full of youthful exuberance and ambition, but having started with 'Bowdens' when he was nineteen, he had gained good experience of the job and understood the local property market. From that point of view, he was just what Simon needed.

The problem, as Simon saw it, was that Bowdens was a big estate agency, with branches in pretty much every town, and matching the security and perks they could offer employees might be difficult. However, when he was with King and Rutter, they had conducted research into that organisation's employment arrangements, before head-hunting a handful of its staff, so he knew that for young men of a certain age, there was one weak point that he could exploit.

'So, I see you are driving one of Bowden's standard issue Vauxhalls,' Simon said. 'Their car policy always was a bit mean.'

'Yeah,' smiled Gary. 'You have to be a Senior to get the choice of a leased car, and until then your choice is just a basic Vauxhall in red, white or blue.'

'What sort of cars do Senior Negotiators get?'

'Well, it is still a bit limited. Fords, Minis, Golfs, that sort of thing. Or better models of Vauxhalls, of course, but nobody chooses those.'

'Not a BMW, then?'

'No chance! You have to be a Branch Manager to get one of them.'

'You know I explained that we would match the Bowdens commission scales and pay a higher basic, with a guaranteed minimum for the first six months?'

'Yes?'

'Well, how would you feel if I added your choice of leased car, with the benchmark being a BMW 120

Sport, or anything in that price bracket you liked, so long as it had four doors?'

'Really?'

'Yes, and as I said we write our own policies here, so we are not tied to any sort of restrictive corporate nonsense. You would start with the job title of Senior Negotiator, and if we do go ahead and open that other branch I was telling you about in a couple of years, you could expect to become the Branch Manager here. How does that sound, Gary?'

'OK! When can I start?'

***

'So, Lena,' said Dr Brown, 'I have heard from the local council covering the area where Andrew grew up. They regard him as a local star, and they want to run an exhibition featuring his work in the Town Hall.'

'That sounds nice.'

'Well, yes, but they originally said they would like Andrew to make a personal appearance, as they are hoping to get the local television people to cover the event.'

'Oh dear. I don't think Andrew would like that.'

'No, of course you are right, but we may have come up with a compromise. How do you think he would react if they came here and spoke to him in his studio? Do you think we could manage something like that?'

'I don't know ...'

'There is another incentive, from Andrew's point of view. They are considering either commissioning him to paint some local landmark or buying one of his works to display in the Town Hall itself permanently.'

'Is difficult, I'm thinking, Dr Brown. But I got idea. How about we ask Andrew to do sketch of his parents' cottage? Maybe use the picture on the estate agent's details when it was sold. I looked it up on Rightmove, and there are some nice views on there from beach.'

'That is a great idea, Lena! I will telephone the Town Hall and see if they would accept that, and then we will see if we can talk Andrew into doing it.'

***

'Susie come round this morning, with little Dicky. She had got this secretary woman coming to see the office, like.'

'Oh yeah?'

'Well, don't sound too keen, Mikey. I might think you were the tiniest bit interested in my job an' what I do all day!'

'Sorry, babe. So what's it all about with this Susie?'

'Susie is Simon's wife, Mikey.'

'Yeah, and the mum of the baby you are in love with. I know that, don't I!'

'Right. Well, this woman, Jenny, 'er name was, might be going to be the office receptionist and that. That would make her my boss, I'm guessing.'

'Oh. Now I see why you was interested.'

'Yeah. Well. Susie only wanted me to look after the baby while she talked to this Jenny, but I could hear what they were sayin', like. You would be surprised how much money they offered her. If I had wages like that, I could buy my own house, rather than just look at pictures of them in the office windows!'

'Well, tha's interestin'. I reckon 'e must have pots of money, that Simon. Y'know I does the windows round the big shops in the town, up the coast?' Karen nodded. 'I do the Mercedes garage, an' Dodgy Dave, what works there cleaning the cars, like, told me your Simon 'as been in there sniffing about. Gotta flash new Merc estate car on order, 'e says!'

'Nah, that's prob'lee a lease, innit. I heard them talkin' about all that. Pay so much a month and look like a millionaire in a posh new car.'

'Flash though.'

'Nothing wrong with your old banger, Mikey. That'll do for us, I reckon.'

'Yeah. Holds special memories for me, that old car does, babe,' winked Mikey. 'If you know what I mean.'

'Shut up! You shut up, Mikey!' said Karen, blushing to her roots.

Chapter 35

Simon knew he needed to tell Susie what he had found out, and he felt pressure to do it soon, rather than later, in case she found out another way.

At least Sir Lemuel's generous offer softened her inevitable horror of staying in the flat, but the story he had to tell was bound to upset her.

He probably shouldn't have told her all the details about Elliot being stabbed and bleeding to death on the kitchen floor of the flat. He couldn't really blame Susie for refusing to spend another night there with the baby, but he got a bit carried away with the drama of it all as he told the story. As a consequence, she had packed up and returned to their house in Thames Ditton to await events, saying that she would not return until their new home was ready, and she was only prepared to accept it if he promised that it was a house where nobody had died.

Simon asked Sir Lemuel about that as he was shown around Elliot's former home, stepping around the decorators and their equipment, but he would only say that it was impossible to be sure, given that people were born, lived and died in houses all the time, and this one was old, Georgian, he thought, so who knew what had gone on there.

It was, however, generous of him to offer them the large house rent-free for another three months to make up for the shock and upheaval that the revelation of the recent history at the flat had caused. The decorators, he said, would be finished in about ten days.

Of course, Susie took the Nissan to drive back to their old home, which, since Simon had returned his company Jaguar SUV to King and Rutter, meant it was necessary to urgently hire a car.

All that was available at short notice locally was a tiny, bright yellow Suzuki with two doors, pop-out back windows, and no air-conditioning. But it was only ten days or so until his brand new Mercedes was due to be delivered, so it would have to do.

Simon was in the process of visiting each of the houses they had for sale to explain the situation and introduce himself, and to encourage each of the owners to stick with the new business, rather than going elsewhere. The noisy little Suzuki did not project the sort of first impression he had imagined making, so he altered his carefully practised opening remarks to include an explanation that the car was just a temporary rental.

There was also a problem with the new shop sign he had intended to order.

The young man who came to measure up and provide an estimate from 'Flag-Up Signage' immediately deflated Simon.

'Well, I'd be delighted to provide you with a lovely big shiny back-lit plastic sign,' he said, 'but this is a conservation area, mate. That sort of thing is not allowed.'

Simon should have realised that there was a reason why all the other shops in the street had painted signs in muted colours. It was something he had missed in all the excitement.

'You could probably put some subtle LED lights around it, I would have thought, but nothing too garish. What colours were you thinking of?'

Bright orange with three-dimensional illuminated black lettering, admitted Simon.

'Oh blimey, no! The Council would never permit that here. What you are going to need is an old-fashioned artisan sign painter to cover up the previous name of the business and paint on a new one. And to avoid a long drawn-out fight with the council, it will probably need to be in the same style and colours as the existing.'

'Oh blast,' said Simon. He could not afford to delay reopening the business while he was arguing petty points with the local council. 'Where could I find somebody like that? Do those sort of skills still exist today?'

'Well, they might. My grandpa did that. He is semi-retired now, of course, but he did most of the sign writing around here back in the day. I wouldn't be surprised if he did the sign you have got up there now, to be honest.'

'And do you think he would do it?'

'Well, I could ask. We could print and produce all your 'for sale' boards, and that, in lightweight foam-filled plastic, if you are interested. Most of the agents around here use us to put them up and take them down, too.'

'Thank you very much,' said Simon halfheartedly, as he realised he would have to rethink the new corporate identity media he had planned for the business, scrapping the orange and black theme, and not just on the signage. To make it all match, he would have to redesign the headed notepaper, business cards, property details, and brochure templates, as well as the graphics on the 'for sale' boards. He urgently needed to call the printer and stop his order.

Elliots 'theme' of pale blue with white lettering, picked out with black edging, would, it seemed, have to be the future style of everything to do with the rebranded and relaunched 'Richards Real Estate' business. He hoped the printer had not started to produce the copious amounts of printed matter he had ordered.

There was one upside that the bank manager at least had approved of.

Elliot did not believe in running his business on credit. Pretty much everything was owned outright and paid for. The only thing on a lease was the old photocopier, and that was going as soon as the state-of-the-art, integrated, full-colour, multi-media, combined digital printing suite, and office copier machine arrived.

Simon had taken out a mortgage against the freehold of the shop to fund the business, of course, and that was covering the costs of setting everything up and getting the business running.

Whilst the 'beech effect' chipboard desks were not up to much, and the blue hessian office chairs were the sort of thing you might be more likely to see in a dentist's waiting room than a modern estate agency, everything included with the 'fixtures and fittings' was at least functional and in reasonable condition. They would do for now, and not having to replace them was a help to the cash flow.

Simon was dubious about the telephone system, however, which looked like something out of the 1980's. But fortunately, Karen seemed to know how it and the antiquated computer system worked.

Thank goodness for Karen.

Chapter 36

'You see, the thing is, it really won't do,' said Panda.

'Put that down, Amanda, and be sensible. The Governor wanted me to remind you that working in the kitchen is a privilege. He feels your recent behaviour doesn't ...'

'Shut up, you fat bitch. Nobody shows me any respect around here. I need to work in the kitchen to get away from these ghastly, stupid women you lock me up with. I'm a hundred times better than any of them, and I deserve better treatment.'

'Well, the Governor says you have to earn these things, Amanda ...'

'My friends call me Panda,'

'Panda then ...'

'Ha! What makes you think you could ever be a friend of mine, you common slug? Why doesn't the Governor come down here himself and explain his petty rules to me?'

'He has sent me ...'

'Is he scared of me? Are you scared of me?'

'What is that you have got there in your hand? Where did you get that? Put it down!'

'Oh, I'll put it down all right ... down your fat squawking throat!'

'Amanda, stop! Get off. Let me go ... No!'

The Deputy Governor reached over and stopped the footage on the monitor.

'So I think you can see how the incident developed and worked out from there, last night, until the other officer came back in and raised the alarm.'

'These new CCTV cameras with sound in the kitchens are good, aren't they? And in colour too! How is the officer now?' asked the Governor.

'Unfortunately, she has lost the sight in one eye and may yet lose the other one. She will be in hospital for some time, I'm told.'

'And she managed to do all that with a plastic fork? For God's sake!'

***

The sun was quite warm as she walked round the

corner and saw the house she wanted. She was pretty sure that was his truck, and there was a burly man in shorts wrestling a large lawnmower into the back.

She was a bit disappointed that DS Curtis hadn't caught her up and was apparently buying cigarettes in the shop on the corner, but this was too good an opportunity to waste, and he might drive off at any moment if she waited.

She stopped behind him and coughed politely.

'Hello? What can I do for you, officer?'

'Mr Todd? Is this your truck?' said WPC Linda Pope. 'Are you aware that you have at least two very bald tyres?'

'Well, no ... I don't use it much, and ...'

'Well, perhaps it might be wise to get it looked at when you have a moment. But that is not why I wanted to speak to you, sir. Am I right that you do regular gardening work for Mr and Mrs Elliot Markham?'

'Did. Not now. He's dead, and she is in prison. I would have thought you knew that.'

'No need to be cheeky. When were you last there?'

***

Now that the weather had improved, it was quite usual to see joggers out at all times of day, but especially in the early morning.

As Karen unlocked the office door, she was surprised to find Simon already inside, out of breath, and dressed in running gear.

'Hi Karen,' he puffed. 'Bit late this morning. Overslept. Just popped in to get my laptop. Going home for a shower, then I'll be in. Sorry.'

'OK,' said Karen. She knew Simon went for a run in the mornings, but had never seen him in his running gear, or out of breath before.

Since Susie had gone back to their house in Thames Ditton, she had noticed that he was not as well-groomed as usual, and she resolved to ask him if he was eating properly, as he bustled past her into the road.

'Shan't be long,' he said.

It occurred to Karen to ask why he needed his laptop if he was going home for a shower, but the moment had passed before she had the chance.

***

Simon was opening the laptop as he got to the flat.

He was already much later than usual and didn't want to completely miss his usual morning ritual of a video call with Susie and little Dicky.

He was missing them terribly, and although it had only been four days, he was beginning to realise how capable Susie was at smoothing out the domestic chaos around their lives since the baby arrived.

He had overslept twice now, and without what had become the usual nocturnal visits to feed or rock the baby back to sleep, when he sometimes kept them awake for what seemed like hours on end, he had no routine to follow. He might have been more rested, but it was surprising how quickly disrupted sleep became normal, and he missed always being alert for any sound from the cot.

Susie was online and answered his call. And there he was … and was that a smile?

Simon felt the tension rolling off him as he gazed at his precious little son.

'Why aren't you up? Why are you still in your running gear?' said Susie. 'We've been up for hours, haven't we, little man!'

Chapter 37

DS Curtis needed to be more certain what Errol Richards had been able to see from his boat, but he did not want to follow the Detective Inspector's suggestion at all.

He was no seaman at the best of times, but the thought of riding the swell just off shore as the tide turned, in a tiny fishing boat which no doubt stank of dead fish and crustaceans, and was probably liberally smeared with their body parts, held no attraction for him at all. So he came up with another plan, and at a little after three o'clock in the afternoon, he was in the pub.

'So, Errol,' he said, as he paid for the drinks at the bar, 'what I'd like you to do is quite simple …'

'Yes, but you got the have the same tide. Otherwise, what you see is different.'

'What sort of tide was it?'

'I'd 'ave to look that up.'

'Aren't they the same every day?'

'No way. They change with the phases of the moon. Didn't they teach you that at school, Detective Sergeant?'

'I was off that day with acute seasickness.'

'Ha, very good. So I take it you want me to video the view so you don't have to come out on my boat and see it for yourself?'

'Very perceptive, Errol … Another beer?'

***

WPC Linda Pope had a suggestion to make.

'Why don't we go down there and look for anything obvious. After all the gardener said he had not been there for several months so, if it is part of a crime scene, with nobody living in the house, it might still be undisturbed.'

'I suppose it is worth a try,' said DI Francis. 'Yes, go ahead. And by the way have we got any further in tracking down the boyfriend? He might have a grudge against Emma Johnson, don't you think?'

'There was nobody at his flat, and according to his employers he has taken three months leave of absence. He might be anywhere.'

'Do you think he might of done a runner, sir? Can

we look into that?' said DS Curtis. 'He is possibly a suspect if what Errol Richards is saying has any truth in it.'

'This is all pretty flimsy stuff, you know. But yes, I suppose we have to check it out.' DI Francis nodded. 'We might need to re-open an investigation into Emma Johnson properly, I agree, but I don't want to do it if we can discretely shut this down now. See if the boyfriend has any friends, workmates or family who might know where he has gone and why, but don't spend more than a couple of days on it. This could all be nothing and Errol Richards might be having a jolly good laugh at our expense.'

***

'Crikey, it's enormous!' said Karen, looking up at Simon as he stood on the low window ledge easing the end out ready to position it. 'I don' think I've ever seen one that big before.'

'I thought you would be impressed, Karen,' said Simon. 'Now try to pull the box clear while I lift it out. It is not heavy, but it is very awkward, and I'd hate to drop it.'

'Don't 'spose you could get EastEnders on it though. There is no aerial in 'ere to plug it into.'

'It is not that sort of television, Karen,' smiled Simon as he eased a bit more out of the box. 'It is officially called a monitor, rather than a telly, and it works with the new computer system. You wait and see what it can do when we get it integrated and working. I think you will be impressed.'

'Hang on, Simon. You've got it the wrong way round, ain'tcha?'

'No, it is supposed to face out onto the street, it is for the customers outside to watch, not us!'

***

'There is someone down there,' said WPC Linda. 'Look, there is a man walking down the path.'

The long sloping garden at Elliot and Panda Markham's house led down towards the cliff edge and the sea beyond. From the ground floor of the house, as you looked out, the wall at the end of the garden was concealed by the rolling lawns, trees, bushes, and flower borders and the drop in levels made it appear that the garden rolled right down to the sea.

'If you didn't know that wall was there,' WPC Linda marvelled, 'it would be a bit like an infinity pool, going out to sea.'

'An optical illusion, Linda? Yes, I see what you mean,' said DS Curtis. 'Come on, let's see if we can catch up with that bloke before he gets down to the end and starts mucking up our potential crime scene.'

'I think it might be Sir Lemuel Fulton-Marks, sir,' Linda broke into a run as she reached the wide brick path in front of them.

'I wonder what he is doing?' DS Curtis was hurrying to catch her up.

Chapter 38

'Nobody seems to have a clue where Peter Jenkins, the boyfriend, has gone, sir.'

'Workmates, family?'

'Nothing,' said DS Curtis. 'The workmates didn't seem very keen on him, and none of them seemed to be close pals with him. They didn't seem very interested in where he was. His boss said the 'leave of absence' form was submitted via their internal computer system, and as he works in a different office, on the other side of London, he simply approved it without seeing the bloke face to face. It seems he was something quite senior, to do with computers or IT, and kept himself to himself.'

'Family-wise, sir,' chipped in Linda, 'there is a sister in Aberdeen, who has not seen him for ten years and doesn't keep in touch, although she is his next-of-kin, and until about three years ago, he had an elderly mother who was in a nursing home near here, until she passed away. He was married, but not divorced, as far as I could establish. No idea where his wife went yet. That is all we could find.'

'Neighbours?'

'Again, it seems he was a very private person. He would nod a greeting if he saw them, but never really spoke to anyone.'

'How did he get to know Emma Johnson then?'

'They were both members of a Yoga class locally. I've spoken to the woman that runs it,' said WPC Linda. 'But she said he was very quiet and didn't mix with them socially.'

'Sounds like a miserable anti-social sod to me,' said DI Francis. 'Nobody has reported him missing, I suppose, so we can't get a search warrant for his flat?'

'No, sir, I suspect he might just be abroad on holiday, perhaps.'

'All right. I suppose we will have to move it up the agenda a bit. Linda, could you look into phone records, his financial stats and all that, please, and can you get his employment history.'

'Yes, sir.'

'Now, tell me what you found down in the fairy dell at the bottom of the Markham's garden … Oh, and have you been out on Errol Richard's boat to see what he saw yet, DS Curtis?'

***

The van unloading the enormous and very heavy printing machine was parked across the entrance to the car park when Simon noticed that someone was sitting in a car patiently waiting to get in.

He went over to apologise to the driver. Presumably, it was one of the occupants of the flats above, he thought.

'I'm very sorry,' he said to the slowly opening darkened glass window on the Mercedes Sports. 'I'm sure we won't be long.'

The face gradually appearing in the window was striking. Dark hair framing a stunning, olive-skinned face, now smiling with perfect, very white teeth.

'Is OK. No rush. I happy to wait,' she said. There was an accent. Italian?

'Sorry,' said Simon. 'Equipment delivery for my new business. Do you live in one of the flats?'

The door of the car was opening, and a slim leg emerged, followed by another, then the elegantly dressed youngish woman unwound herself from the low car and stood up.

'Si. Is no problem. You work the new business?'

Simon was temporarily unable to speak as he took in the shapely vision before him. She looked like a fashion model, although she might be a little shorter than the usual catwalk queens. She was, Simon thought, quite simply gorgeous.

'Er, yes. Well, I own the business, actually,' said Simon, involuntarily drawing in his stomach and inflating his chest as he held out his hand. 'Simon Hamilton-Smythe. How do you do?'

'Mucho ... is nice meet you too. Teresa. I living top floor,' she touched Simon's hand briefly and smiled even more broadly.

'Right. Well, yes. I'm sure we won't hold you up much longer. Have you lived here long?'

'Yes, but no. I live mostly the ... er, Spain. No here much.'

That was a pity, thought Simon. He could put up with a lot of seeing this beauty around.

'I've only just moved here myself. From Surrey, you know, when I bought the business.'

'Si? Is sad the Elliot, no? He nice man, always help me.'

I bet he did, thought Simon.

'Help you?'

'Yays. He make carry the cases. Is many stairs. I like him, and Panda, of course.'

'Unfortunately, I never met them.'

'No? But you know is all very sad, yes?'

'Well, I didn't really know what had happened until recently, when Elliot's father-in-law told me ...'

'You know Lemmy? I know him. He ... how you say? He charming. We do the business with him in Spain.'

'You do the business? I mean you know him?'

'Yays. He buy the flats we selling.'

Simon's professional ears pricked up. Was she selling flats? Maybe he could help with that.

'You are in the property business?' he tried.

'Si. Well, is my husband company. We do the ... the making development in Spain. Many flats we got.'

'I see,' said Simon. King and Rutter had once got involved in selling flats in a new development in Spain, and he wondered if it was the same sort of thing.

'Oh, the van. Maybe is finish?' she was saying,

looking over his shoulder.

***

'Thank goodness the DI has given us permission to get on with his Emma Johnson case properly at last,' said DS Curtis. 'If he had beaten around the bush any longer, all the leaves would have come off, and any clues would be long gone.'

When they caught up with Sir Lemuel Fulton-Marks on the wide garden path, they had established that he was only there to put a new padlock on the back gate. Nothing suspicious there, with the house being empty.

Without revealing why they were there, they managed to persuade him to allow them to install the padlock and to inspect the gate's security for him. Because he seemed to be in a rush, he was happy to let them do it, especially when WPC Linda convinced him they were just doing the rounds of properties in the district, keeping an eye on any empty houses.

'That bit about the Police looking out for opportunities for squatters to get in was good, Linda,' chuckled DS Curtis. 'As if we would have time to do anything like that.'

'Yes, but he seemed to swallow it, and it kept him from trampling all over our potential crime scene down here.'

'Yes. Well done. There is quite a lot of mud down here, isn't there. Quite a few tyre tracks as well.'

'Clay soil, you see. It holds its shape for months, years even, when you sculpt it. The gardener's truck had two very bald tyres at the back. He shouldn't have been driving it like that.'

'Yes, I think that must be his tyre tracks.'

'Hold on though … look. There are some others. Chunky tyres made those, and much newer than the ones on that old truck by the look of things.'

'Oh, yes. I think we had better get some photographs of those, Linda, before they get scuffed away.'

'Not much chance of that, by the look of things. I don't think anyone has been down here for months. Look at all those leaves piled up against the wall. They must be from last autumn.'

'How did you know about the properties of clay soil, Linda?'

'Pottery classes.'

Chapter 39

Andrew was uncomfortable and couldn't keep still. He hated this sort of thing and fervently wished he had not let Dr Brown and Lena talk him into it.

The 'crew', as they called themselves, had set up big silver umbrellas to deflect light in the windows of his studio, and wires were trailing everywhere. It was made worse, Andrew complained, when some of the 'crew' took out pasties and proceeded to drop flakes of pastry on the floor.

But there was one compensation. There was a short, bearded man with one of those clapper things, who wrote something down on the board and then said 'Cut!' or 'Rolling!' as they filmed. He had an interesting face, and Andrew wanted to sketch him.

'Well, that is very nice of you,' said the man. 'I can get you some press photographs to work off if you like …'

'No, I want to draw you here, with all this mess in place, in my studio.'

Sid, for that was his name, had been briefed about

what Andrew was like and his unusual behaviour, and remembered that he must humour him to keep him sweet.

'OK, Andrew. How about I get our photographer to take some pictures of me that you can use as a reference? You can see them on his screen and choose which you like for us to print off for you.'

Andrew had liked that idea, and he effectively turned the tables on the 'crew' by directing them to take photographs for him of Sid standing here or there, and in this or that pose. Then, Andrew had them working almost as much for him, as doing what they were actually there to do.

Watching proceedings from the door, Dr Brown and Lena shared a smile. This was going to be a success after all.

***

WPC Linda's phone rang in her pocket, and she answered it swiftly with one hand.

'It's Trisha,' she said. 'She has been looking through the stuff Emma Johnson left in that mobile home she was staying in. She has found a letter from a solicitor that Emma used, which she thinks we might be interested in.'

'Uh, huh,' said DS Curtis, continuing to study the top of the wall.

'What have you got?' asked Linda and listened as Trisha explained. 'He might, yes. Good work. Well spotted. We will follow that up when we get back.'

'What was that all about?' asked DS Curtis.

'There is a letter from this solicitor setting out his fees and so on, and it starts by saying "following my conversation with our client Peter Jenkins" and says something about him recommending them for Emma to use. Trisha thinks if this Jenkins is his client, he might know where he is.'

'Well, that is good work, Linda! Come on, there is not much more to see here, we should get back and check it out.'

'Better put Sir Lemuel's padlock on the gate first …'

'Good point,' said DS Curtis, drawing it out of his pocket.

***

As Teresa parked her Mercedes Sports, Simon approached her again and asked if she would be interested in having a look around his new office, perhaps with a cup of tea.

'You got coffee?' she asked, and when Simon nodded, she said, 'OK is date. Then maybe you give me help get suitcase upstairs?'

Simon, of course, was delighted to oblige and trotted along behind her as she glided through the back door of the office, like her faithful Labrador.

He was more careful than the average dog following a scent, however, and did not let his tongue hang out.

***

Errol Richards was chuckling happily at the bar.

'Wha's tickling you, Errol?' asked the barman.

'I just seen old Ted, the sign writer.'

'Oh yes?'

'He's doing a new name plate on one of our boats. Lovely job he makes o' them.'

'Well, why is it funny?'

''E told me he's got to paint up a new sign for the Elliots office, now the new bloke's got it,' Errol took a deep slug of his beer. 'An' the funny thing is they're naming it after me!'

'What?'

'S'gonna be called "Richards Real Estate" innit. My mum's gonna be so proud!'

Chapter 40

'There is a limit as to what I can tell you, as you know, Detective Sergeant. Client confidentiality.'

'Of course, I fully understand, sir, but if you could just confirm whether Peter Jenkins is a client of yours ...'

'As I said, there is no secret about that ...'

'Well, the problem is that he has taken a leave of absence from work, and we have no idea where to contact him, you see.'

'And why do you need to contact him?'

'Well, that is where I hit the "confidentiality" buffers, sir. It is nothing against him. He is not in any trouble or anything; we are just anxious to contact him to see if he can give us some information.'

'I see. Well, perhaps I could get a message to him for you, if you like, and ask him to contact you, if he wants to.'

'Well, that would be most helpful if you could, sir. Just out of interest, have you spoken to him recently?'

'He is alive and well, if that is what is concerning you, and I suppose it wouldn't hurt to say that he is on an extended visit to Spain.'

'Is he? I mean, thank you. If you could ask him to contact us, that would be really helpful, sir.'

'Always happy to help the Police, Detective Sergeant ...'

'I'll bet you are,' mumbled DS Curtis after the call disconnected.

***

'So, do you have an agent promoting your developments in England, Teresa?' Simon asked.

'Er, no ...'

Simon sat up straight in his chair. He had no experience of selling property in Spain, but he could soon find someone who did, and split fees with them, if there was a chance here.

'Is no possible just a now ...'

'Oh?'

'My husband and a me padre, my father, they sort it out. I maybe come to England for long time, till is more better.'

'Is there a problem then?'

'Si. Is big problem. Many months. Police and everything doing the looking. Is big mix-up. My ... my father he say me, go the England, keep out of it.'

'Right,' Simon was thinking quickly. This didn't sound good. Perhaps it would be better if he changed the subject.

'So, whereabouts in Spain do you come from?' he asked.

***

'Well, Elliot drove a Range Rover, didn't he? I saw it at the golf club.'

'So I believe, sir.'

'Well, that explains your knobbly tyre prints then, doesn't it?'

'No, sir, with respect, these were not made by a Chelsea tractor type of thing,' said WPC Linda. 'These are more serious off-road tyres, we think, and pretty much new, if you ask me.'

'Has the gardener got any other vehicles, do you think? Could it be another of his, or a rotavator or something?'

'Too wide a footprint for a rotavator,' said DS Curtis.

'And Mr Todd only has one vehicle registered to his name, sir, and I've found out that it is currently uninsured.'

'What does Peter Jenkins drive?'

'A Skoda Octavia, sir, and it's parked at the back of his flat.'

DI Francis sighed. 'Oh, all right. Pull the gardener in and see if he can throw any light on it, but try to keep it low-key. I still think Errol might be inventing all this.'

'Yes, sir,' said DS Curtis and WPC Pope in unison.

***

'What have you got in here? Gold bars?' Simon was puffing as he got the big, heavy case to the top of the stairs, but Teresa didn't laugh at his joke.

'Thanks,' she said. 'Is most a kind of you. Maybe see you around soon.'

Simon felt as if he had been dismissed. She certainly wasn't making any attempt to open her front door while he was there, so he wished her well, said if there was anything she needed, she knew where he was, and made his way back down the stairs.

Gary Kirby was pulling into the car park as he reached the ground floor.

'Can't stop, Simon,' he said through his driver's window. 'Just wanted to let you know that I have put in my resignation letter this morning. Must dash, I'm late for an appointment.'

Simon's deflated ego rose again as he went back into the office to tell Karen the good news.

***

The large-format sketch pad Andrew placed on the kitchen table was open to what he considered to be the best of his efforts.

'Is perfect, Andrew! The Council people gonna love this. Well done.'

'Well, not quite perfect yet, but not too bad for a start. Do you think they would accept it as it is if I tidy it up a bit, Lena? Is it big enough for what they want?'

'I dunno. I ask Dr Brown to find out. Can I take a picture of this on my phone and send it to him?'

'If you like. I really don't have to go back there if I do this, do I, Lena?'

'No, Andrew, you don't have to go back there, I promise.'

***

When the gardener visited the police station to make his statement, WPC Linda Pope was amused to see that he had walked there.

'Not taking any chances with your truck then, Mr Todd.'

'Well, before you start, I've renewed my insurance now, and I admit it slipped my mind, and my mate is sorting out some new tyres for me as we speak.'

'Excellent. Now then, do you recognise these tyre tracks?' DS Curtis showed him the pictures on Linda's phone.

'Should I?'

'Well, you are the guy with the tyre issues,' said Linda. 'Any clue how they got there at the bottom of Mr and Mrs Markham's garden?'

'Well, as you know, I could never afford big chunky tyres like that, so it certainly wasn't me, but beyond that, I can't help you. They look like the sort of thing you see on old school Land Rovers or that sort of thing, but I can't see who would want to take one of them down that garden unless they were delivering something. I drive my truck … well, I *drove* my truck down there when I needed to move my mowers and that, when I was employed there, but that is all.'

'The path is wide enough for you to get down there?'

'Well, you have seen it. It is certainly much wider than the average garden path. More like a sort of brick road, really. I had to repair a bit of it once, where the frost lifted a part of the surface, and I can tell you it was built to last. More like a Roman road than a garden path.'

'Well, that is very helpful, Mr Todd. Thank you for your time, and for … for walking down here.'

When Linda returned to the interview room after seeing Mr Todd out, DS Curtis had a question.

'Well, Linda, we know Peter Jenkins doesn't drive a 4x4 and putting aside whatever he is up to in Spain, apart from the fact that he didn't actually ever bother getting a divorce before he took up with Emma Johnson, he is looking pretty clean. If we could get to speak to him, and if we find out if he has an alibi for the time of her death, we are going to have to cross him off our suspects list. Now, who does that leave us with?'

'Nobody.'

'Yes, you are correct, of course. A big fat nobody.'

'Oh dear,' said Linda.

DS Curtis took a packet of cigarettes out of his pocket and shook one out, placing it between his lips.

'You can't light that in here, sir!'

'I know that. Shit, Linda, we've got nothing. I'm going outside for a smoke.'

Chapter 41

WPC Linda Pope had nothing much to do, so she decided to call in and see how Karen was getting on in her new job, and what she thought of her new boss.

On the way, she took a call from her old school friend, Jenny West, and listened to her excited babble about being offered a new job at the office she was coincidentally on her way to visit.

'I can't wait! And you wouldn't believe the money they are offering! Fantastic. I'm even going to have an office junior working for me ...'

'As it happens, I think I know your office junior, and by some strange bit of serendipity, I am actually on my way to see her now.'

'To arrest her? What has she done?'

'No, certainly not to arrest her, Jenny! Karen is a charming young girl, and, unusually these days, for someone her age, I don't think she has a dishonest bone in her body. Do they know you have accepted the job?'

'Well, I have accepted it, but she probably won't know that yet.'

'So, can I tell her all about you?'

'Well, I 'spose … Wait! Not everything about me, Linda!'

'OK, Jenny, here is the deal. I will only tell her nice things about you today. But if I hear you have been nasty to her, I'll tell her all the things you got up to at school!'

***

'So the Centenary event at the Town Hall is on Friday, Andrew, as you know. The plan is to unveil your drawing and open the exhibition of your work in time for the early evening local TV news.' Dr Brown settled himself a little more comfortably on the old sofa. 'Lena and I are going to watch it here with you, if that is all right.'

'There won't be any more reporters, will there?'

'No, Andrew, it will just be us watching it on the television. Lena has got some of your favorite biscuits that we can have while we are watching, if you like.'

'OK, Dr Brown.'

Peter Jenkins unexpectedly telephoned DS Curtis on his private mobile number that afternoon and was able to confirm that he was alive and well. But he had much more to say.

He laughed when DS Curtis asked if he would mind confirming what he was doing on the morning of Emma Johnson's death.

'No problem with that, I was in a hotel in York, about to go to a conference related to work,' he said.

He assured DS Curtis that his department head could confirm he was there, as they had breakfast together at approximately the time Emma set off for her run.

DS Curtis apologised and explained that he was tasked with just tying up a few loose ends before the file was put to bed, and whilst he was sorry to trouble Peter, clarifying one or two things would tie it all up, he said.

His relaxed, friendly manner led him to believe that maybe Peter thought they knew one another. He might have thought his solicitor had asked him to call because he knew who DS Curtis was. He made no bones about admitting straight away that he and Emma had had an affair, but it had ended when she was arrested for the manslaughter of Elliot

Markham, and he had not seen her since.

'That has cleared that up. Thank you,' said DS Curtis. 'I assumed that was how it was, but I needed to check to put a bow on the paperwork. Sorry to trouble you with it.'

'No problem. I know how you policemen like to tie up loose ends, especially when somebody has died. Now, as it happens, you might, ah, that is to say, it is possible that you may come across my wife there, in the town, I mean, at some point, Mike.'

Mike? thought DS Curtis, and wondered how Peter had got it into his head that his name was Mike. Nobody called him Mike, mostly because his name was Mark.

'She is back there from Spain. There won't be any need to tell her about this? About Emma, I mean, will there?'

DS Curtis was taken aback.

'No, of course not, Peter, but I thought you were separated from your wife?'

'Thank you, Mike. Teresa and I... It is complicated, you see. My wife is Spanish, as you know, and Spain is a very Catholic country, where divorce is not something they ...'

DS Curtis realised that Peter Jenkins thought he

was either talking to somebody else or that they knew each other in some way. He decided not to disillusion him and to just listen and see where it went.

'Why exactly are you in Spain, Peter, if your wife is here, if you don't mind me asking?'

'Well, I daresay you have all the information about the Court case at your fingertips from the Spanish authorities, so I won't bore you, but the fraud hearing has been brought forward, and of course, I have to be here for that.'

DS Curtis had no idea what this was all about, but he decided it might be wise to give the impression that he knew something about what was happening, to see if he could gain an insight into the situation.

'My information is probably a little out of date,' he said. 'We provincial folk seem to be quite low down the mailing list for updates. Perhaps you could bring me up to speed.'

'Of course, Mike. I say, we have actually spoken before, haven't we? I just naturally assumed you are one of the investors that Lemmy Fulton-Marks bought on board?'

'Uh-huh,' said DS Curtis carefully, fascinated by how this was panning out. Now, Sir Lemuel Fulton-Marks seemed to be involved in some way. He let the conversation run on.

'Sorry, didn't mean to be rude, but one meets so many people ... although my lawyer in London wouldn't have asked me to contact you if you weren't "on side" as it were, so forgive me for being a bit cautious.'

'No offence taken, Peter.'

'Now that I know who you are, we can speak candidly, so obviously, on the understanding that this goes no further ... You will remember that the leaders of the timeshare owners group action had been granted an initial hearing, and the judiciary decided to take it forward to the next stage? We all thought nothing would happen until next year, but for some reason, the Spanish Courts have decided to bring the whole thing forward, and we had to present our case in detail a few weeks ago. We have been told the case will probably take about two weeks to resolve, but no doubt you know what the Spanish are like for dragging things out, hence my three months' leave of absence.'

'I see, and how is it all going?'

DS Curtis began to relax. As far as he could make out, Peter Jenkins and his wife might have bought a timeshare apartment and were involved in suing the developers to get some money back in a group action. Perhaps Peter thought that this "Mike" he had been talking to had bought one too.

All this was fairly common in Spain, from what he had heard. Peter and his wife may have been duped into buying something that hadn't worked out as they thought, it was hardly crime of the century. But there was more.

'Well,' Peter was explaining, 'The blasted timeshare owners' residents association have got involved with some national group who represent loads of other people who bought timeshare, and then listened to their chiselling Spanish lawyers, all acting in consortium and backing us up against the wall. We are sure we are safe enough, though. Our Spanish lawyers say our contract is rock solid and the timeshare owners won't see a penny.'

The penny dropped for DS Curtis. He wasn't speaking to a defrauded timeshare buyer, he was talking to one of the people who potentially defrauded them. The other side of the coin, as it were. And all the while, Peter Jenkins made no bones about holding down quite a senior job at HMRC. Some side hustle!

'But Pedro thought it might be wise to send Teresa away, given that she did most of the actual face-to-face selling,' Peter continued. 'So that is why she is over there in her flat, but the daft bitch has lost her phone, so we can't contact her. I've told Pedro that they don't stand a chance of winning, so there is nothing to worry about, but when Teresa and I first separated, he bought her that flat over there, and as she has kept it ever since. He thought she would be off the radar there.'

'Right,' said DS Curtis. He was struggling to take this all in, but he smelled a rat and thought the time for decisive action had arrived. 'What is her address here, Peter? If you like, I could pop in and see if she is OK?'

'Oh, I say, would you, Mike? As I said, Teresa lost her mobile phone at the airport, on the plane, or somewhere, she thinks. And of course, the phone in the flat was cut off ages ago, so unless she calls Pedro, or in the unlikely event that she calls me, we have no idea how she is. And naturally, we don't want the Spanish authorities getting wind of where she is and coming chasing after her.

'No problem, Peter, I'll drop by.'

'Thanks ever so much, Mike. I was going to ask Lemmy, but as you are on the spot ... And, by the way, please don't worry, your money is quite safe, and the second phase of the development will be starting as soon as this little difficulty is all out of the way. As you probably know, there are quite a lot of policemen like you amongst our investors. Lemmy seems to know a whole lot of you chaps. And obviously, policemen are not going to get involved in anything underhanded. It is all quite open and above board, so stick with us, Mike, and you will soon be reaping the rewards, I can promise you.'

'That is good to know, Peter.'

'Look, if there is nothing else, I'd better go, these international mobile calls cost a fortune … Ah, yes, and the address of my wife's flat is Flat 2, 15a Cliff Road, by the way.'

As soon as he finished the mobile call, DS Curtis called the Chief Inspector's office on his desk phone and asked to see him. International fraud needs to be moved up the chain of command, and quickly.

Chapter 42

DS Curtis threw himself into his office chair and slapped his desk with his hand.

'Dare we ask how it went with the Chief Inspector?' asked Linda.

'There might be another murder soon here, Linda. When I get my hands on that slimy, shirking, slinking Detective Inspector Francis, look out!'

'What has happened?'

'You remember that Panda Markham gouged out a prison officer's eyes not long ago?'

'How can I ever forget?'

'Well, of course, there has been a closed investigation in the prison and an internal review, and there is going to be a court case next week to review her sentence ... and someone has to go and tell her father and ask if he wants to be there.'

'Go on.'

'The boss can't do it because he goes on holiday tonight, and DI Bloody Francis has oiled out of it by claiming his flexitime to take his wife shopping. So guess who has to do it.'

'Well, it won't be that bad, will it? He knows there has been an incident in the prison, doesn't he?'

'Oh yes, it will. Y'see, the details of precisely what she did were held back pending the inquiry, so someone ... and you can guess who, has got to go and see Sir Lemuel Fulton-Marks with the file, and bring him up to speed on all the gory details of what his precious little girl has been up to while detained at His Majesty's pleasure. And then I've got to invite him to come to court to hear it all laid out in public. Next time, remind me not to tell anybody when I uncover an international fugitive living on Cliff Road, so that the Chief can't "volunteer" me for anything else!'

'Whoops,' said Linda. 'Want me to come with you?'

***

'So we can move in tomorrow, Susie. The decoration is all finished.'

'That is great, Simon. I'll start packing. It looks like a really nice house in the pictures you sent me.'

'Yes, but don't get too attached to it. It is only for

three months, and we couldn't afford a big house like that normally.'

'No, I get that. Oh, by the way, those people who came yesterday want a second viewing of our house.'

'Excellent!'

***

'I had a look through the internal telephone lists for you, Linda,' said Trisha, back in the office. 'The nearest I could get was a Detective Mike Kerston, who was briefly based in the old hub further up the coast before they combined it with ours.'

'Well, I suppose Mike Kerston does sound a bit like Mark Curtis. Is he still about?'

'Not any more. He took early retirement and went off to live somewhere in Spain, according to the office busybody in admin, at the hub.'

'Thanks, Trisha. That is very helpful.'

***

Mikey turned round and announced to those in the office, where he was cleaning the inside of the windows, that something odd was happening.

'Look! Police cars, and lots of them.'

'There is one pulling into our car park,' said Simon. 'What's that all about?'

'There are, like, three out the front,' said Karen, peeping around Mikey's substantial frame. 'We ain't on fire or nuffin, are we?'

Outside on his grandson's mobile scaffold tower, old Tom stopped scraping the painted letters off the Elliots shop sign and watched several uniformed police officers getting out of the cars and approaching. One was pressing the intercom buttons on 15a, next door.

Looking again out of the rear-facing window of the private office, Simon was dismayed to see Gary Kirby trying to pull into the car park in his white Vauxhall, only to be turned away by a burly policeman who took up position, stopping anyone from getting in.

Simon reached for his mobile as it rang on his desk.

'What's going on? asked Gary. 'A policeman has just turned me away from the carpark and there is nowhere else to park.'

'I saw that, Gary,' said Simon. 'At present, we have no idea what is happening. Can I suggest you wait in your car up by the recreation ground and as soon as we know …'

'Suffin' is 'appening,' called Karen. 'They are

bringing out that foreign woman from the flats up top ... and she has got handcuffs on!'

***

'Look,' said DS Curtis, as they pulled up on the long drive leading to the farmhouse.

'What am I looking at?' said WPC Linda Pope.

'There is his Land Rover, Linda. Look at the tyres.'

'Of course,' said Linda. 'We didn't think of that. How about I sneak over and take some pictures of them while you go and ring the bell?'

'Yes, do. But when you think about it, why wouldn't he drive down his daughter's and son-in-law's garden in that?'

'Or to put it another way, why would he drive down their garden in his farm truck?'

'I'll go and ring the bell, and you take the pictures. I'll waffle till you come in, and then we will tell him about his daughter and break his heart.'

'Good luck, Mark.' Linda squeezed his arm before opening the car door.

Chapter 43

'There you are,' said WPC Linda, handing her phone to DI Francis. 'Typical flint cut that is. The soil around here is full of them.'

'I don't think I ...'

'And,' said DS Curtis, also handing *his* phone to DI Francis, 'There it is on the tracks we took pictures of down at the bottom of the Elliots' garden.'

'The same cut,' said Linda triumphantly. 'Got him!'

DI Francis held one phone in each hand and then gave them back.

'Well, not necessarily. It doesn't prove he killed Emma Johnson, does it.'

'No, sir,' said DS Curtis. 'But we did a series of the usual "elimination" interviews at the time, after the death, including one from Sir Lemuel, who said he was out on his farm somewhere. We also took one from the owner of the cafe, on the beach.'

'Go on?'

'Well,' said Linda, 'At that time, we were sure it was suicide, so we didn't study them too hard or make the connection; we were just going through the motions. But on looking at them again, there is something ...'

'The owner of the cafe was just opening up at the time of her fall,' DS Curtis took up the story. 'The cafe faces the other way, towards the little carpark behind the beach huts, so he would not have seen her fall, or seen Emma running by. But he did say it was too early for customers and he spends his time preparing the breakfast rolls and so on to be ready, before he opens.'

'In his statement,' added Linda, 'he says that, as usual, there was nobody about at that time and the cafe was still shut, but someone drove into the little car park.'

'He said the chap sat there for a minute or two, looking at his watch,' said DS Curtis. 'He didn't stay long and must have realised that the cafe was not open, so he drove off, he said.'

'We went to see him again just now, sir, and he said he thought the vehicle might have been a green Land Rover.'

***

'It looks great,' said Susie, as soon as Karen had the baby settled in her arms. 'You must have worked really hard.'

'Not me,' said Gary. 'Karen and Simon did most of it, and then Jenny came in, in the evenings, and helped get everything ready for the opening.'

'Gary is still officially working out his notice,' said Simon. 'But he has been backwards and forwards and went to get all the sparkling wine and orange juice and so on from the supermarket for us.'

'And the glasses we hired,' said Jenny. 'And please don't forget Karen and I will want help washing all those up when this is over, guys!'

'Yes,' said Simon, 'I promise not to sneak off! Now, as you know, there is a Centenary event up at the town hall, so quite a few people will probably go to that first. In fact, Sir Lemuel Fulton-Marks is coming on when he can get away from there, and I've asked him to say a few words to declare the business open …'

'Who got all these little nibbles and so on?' asked Susie, impressed.

'I got some from the supermarket,' said Jenny. 'But the Council probably beat me to it and bought them all up for their centenary thing.'

'So my mum and I made the rest,' said Karen, blushing.

'Look alive,' said Gary, 'I think we might be getting our first customer!'

***

'So here we all are,' said Lena. 'I'm excited, Andrew, are you?'

'Well …'

'Hush!' said Dr Brown, resuming his seat between them with the plate of biscuits. 'The local news is starting.'

***

'So I am proud to be able to invite you all here this evening to celebrate one hundred years of the Town Council, here in this building, and to be able to introduce you to our exhibition of local art, featuring, of course, our most famous son, Andrew Gurney. Andrew can't be with us in person this evening, but he has generously presented us with an original artwork to display in the entrance foyer, which celebrates our maritime and fishing heritage, and that will be unveiled shortly, live on the television!' There was a pause for some clapping. 'But in the meantime, can I ask you to raise your glasses in a toast to celebrate one hundred years of the Town Council in this lovely old building!

There was a commotion by the entrance, and one of the more enterprising TV cameramen swung his lens towards the doors.

Accompanied by two uniformed officers and one WPC, Detective Sergeant Mark Curtis strode through the little crowd towards Sir Lemuel Fulton-Marks.

'Could I have a word, sir?' he said, before the cameras cut, and the presenter, back at the studio, filled the screen for those watching at home.

***

'The thing I'm not understanding is his motive,' said DI Francis.

'Well, sir, following my chat a little earlier with him, I think I can throw some light on that. He explained that even before the latest incident, when she blinded the prison officer, he thought Panda was so full of hatred that she would do something terrible when she got out of prison. For Sir Lemuel, it has always been about his grandsons, the twins, you see.'

'He doesn't think she would hurt them, does he?'

'No, sir, quite the opposite. You see, he thinks that Panda holds Emma responsible for killing Elliot, and that when she got out, she might have gone after her. He wanted to get Emma out of the way so that Panda could not hurt her, or even kill her, and end up back in prison. Remember, Emma was killed a while before all this latest stuff happened. His motivation, in killing Emma, back then, sir, was to try to give Panda the chance to be a mother to the boys when she was released, since now they have no father.'

'What family values! Kill or be killed. I wonder how those twins will turn out with Panda as a mother, with all that pent-up rage in her. You read the report I left on your desk about her getting into fights and trying to set the kitchen on fire in the prison, I take it? The blinding was not the first incident. It seems the other inmates are all scared silly of her.'

'I did read that, sir, yes, before the Chief Constable sent me to see her father and explain what she had done on your behalf.'

'Oh yes, of course. Sorry about that.'

DS Curtis gritted his teeth and shook his head. They could talk about that one at another time.

'At least, if she is up to that sort of thing while she is inside, she is not likely to get early release or parole any time soon.'

'Maybe, after this, by the time she gets out, those boys will be old enough to look after themselves and won't need their mother.'

'We can but hope so, sir.'

'Right, Detective Sergeant. Let's go and read Sir Lemuel Fulton-Marks his rights.'

***

It was old Tom who told him how the beach hut came to be called 'Manilla'.

Simon had stopped for a chat as he was taking the cardboard boxes, which had contained the new itegrated digital phone system, to the bin. Old Tom was repainting the 'Sponsored By' boards to go around the boundary at the cricket club, in the scruffy garage, in the car park.

As the new managing agent responsible for the beach huts, Simon had followed Elliots system and written to each of the families who leased the little structures, year after year, to ask if they wanted to renew for another season.

It had taken some time to get a reply, but eventually he had a letter from one woman who explained that her grandfather had rented the hut for many years. Now he had passed away, and whilst it held many happy memories of visiting as a small girl for her, she had moved away and had no children of her own, so would not need it.

Old Tom explained that he had painted the little sign over the door many years previously at the request of the woman's grandfather, and he remembered the family fondly.

The name, he said, has been chosen because the then very small girl had stated that the creamy yellow hut was the same colour as her favorite ice cream, and the closest she could get to pronouncing it was 'Manilla'.

That evening Simon went down through the gate at the bottom of his garden onto the cliff path, and walked down to the beach hut carrying his toolbox.

Once there, after a bit of a struggle, he managed to remove the rusty screws and took down the little nameplate.

It would probably fit in one of those manila envelopes in the office, he thought. He would send it off with a 'Richards Real Estate' compliments slip, as a memento to remember her grandfather by, before old Tom repainted the beach hut for re-letting.

***

Thank you for reading.

***

Here is an extract from another Bob Able title:-

Auntie Caroline's Last Case

In the year since she moved to Ballybunion on the Irish coast, Pauline Patrick, retired and recently widowed Legal Executive, had settled into her little cottage around the corner from the golf links hotel, and acquired a small elderly dog from a rescue centre.

The dog insisted on its walk early each morning and Pauline had devised a clever route in a figure of eight, taking in an element of the path known as the 'Wild Atlantic Way 'but passing close enough to the cottage to give up and go home half way round the perimeter of the golf course section, if the dog became too tired to continue on inclement days, or when his arthritis troubled him.

The section of the walk they both enjoyed most was where the path dropped down steeply onto a sandy cove known locally as 'Ladies Beach', which was sheltered from the wind but usually deserted, at least this early in the morning.

It was on this little beach that the dog suddenly took it into its head to pull away from her and tear off down to the sea to investigate something which had obviously washed up there during the night.

Although she called repeatedly, the dog would not come away and Pauline had to trek down the sand to the water's edge, to re-capture her wilful little pet.

As she approached she saw that what was interesting the dog looked like a bundle of old clothes tied together with thin blue nylon rope. But as she got closer the bundle took on a more recognisable shape.

The body, for that is what it was, had obviously been in the water for a few days, but the disturbing thing was that the wrists and ankles had been tied together at the back so that the corpse assumed a kneeling position and, as the dog pulled at a bit of what looked like the hood of a raincoat, a neat round hole in the back of the almost hairless skull was revealed, which made it obvious that the cause of death was being shot in the head from behind.

Pauline fought down the urge to scream as she caught and re-attached the lead to the dog, and forced herself to stay calm as she reached into her pocket for her mobile phone and dialled the emergency services number.

-ooo0oo-

Bobbie looked around her. They had both been so

contented in the scruffy, but conveniently situated flat they rented on the Richmond Road in Kingston-on-Thames on the outskirts of London. In the months since Rosy, Bobbie's university friend and original flatmate, had moved out and Pedro had moved in, their lives had taken on a sort of gentleness which deepened their love and increased their commitment to each other daily.

Pedro was always very attentive and courteous and did his best to do his share of the chores and cleaning, especially when Bobbie was involved in her work as a trainee investigative journalist or needing to get her head down to study, particularly now that her postgraduate course was coming to an end.

The only fly in the ointment of this idyll was the gradually failing health of Bobbie's Auntie Caroline, who, as an established and rather well-connected investigative journalist, had employed Bobbie, paid for her training, and now involved her in running her business as a partner. Caroline had been given a year to live nine months ago, and had insisted that Bobbie stay in London to complete her course while she returned to her beloved cottage in Scotland.

Bobbie now commuted backwards and forwards between this Scottish house and London and spent as much time as she was able at her Aunt's side, learning the finer points of investigative journalism and, when her aunt was well enough, going with her to meet some of the myriad and fascinating connections she had developed over her long career. Bobbie hoped to be able to depend on some of those contacts when her aunt passed away, and when she took on sole responsibility for the business they were building.

Following several high-profile investigations, which had led to some great press coverage and the sale of their stories through Button and Cohen, the international news agency, the business was in fine shape, and now Bobbie had rather more potential stories to investigate than she could handle.
She was not very interested when she received an email from her friend Henry, at the news agency, tipping her off about the discovery of a body on a beach somewhere in southern Ireland.

She forwarded the email to her aunt in case she had any comment to make, but almost immediately received a follow-up email from Henry to say that the body had been identified as someone called Eoin O'Grady.

The name meant nothing to Bobbie, but she dutifully forwarded the second email to her aunt and thought no more about it.

Moments later, however, her mobile phone rang, and she found that her aunt was very interested in this story indeed.

-ooOoo-

Bobbie was able to answer her aunt's question as to how the body was so swiftly identified following another email from the ever-vigilant Henry.

His latest message explained that the authorities found a wallet with a driving licence, twenty-five euros and some credit cards in the victim's trouser pocket and a payslip in another pocket in his coat.

'Why are you so interested in this chap? 'Bobbie asked.

'I've met him, albeit briefly and years ago. He was a contact who put me onto a really big story.'

'What was that?'

'You remember that night in your flat when you asked me to tell you a scary bedtime story, and I told you about what happened to me during "the troubles" in Ireland? Well, he gave me the tip to meet the skipper of the boat running the guns. He was a junior crew member.'

Bobbie recalled the incident with great clarity. She had no idea until that point what dangerous situations her Auntie Caroline had found herself in before that story was told, and she remembered it almost word for word.

'On the seventh of February 1987, I was in Dublin,' Caroline had said.

'We had gone to a cinema where we planned to meet someone who said he could fix a meeting for us with Adrian Hopkins, who was the skipper of a ship that we were pretty certain was running guns from Libya to the IRA in Ireland. We were right about him, but it took almost a year for the authorities to catch him, and this was pretty much at the beginning of our investigations into his activities.'

'Guns?' Bobbie had asked in astonishment.

'Yes. I worked for a big newspaper group in those days in a team who were involved in all sorts of things. Anyway, as I was saying, we turned up at this old cinema which was all closed up, and there was nobody around, so we wandered round to the back to see if our contact was there. It was just as well we did because, as we went behind the back wall, there was one hell of an explosion that blew out the whole front of the cinema.'

'Oh, my goodness! I remember that story,' Bobbie said now. 'And that is why you had to go and live in that safe house we visited in London, isn't it?'

'Yes, pretty much. Eoin O'Grady was small fry and his tip-off didn't produce the results we were hoping for as the meeting with his boss never actually took place, but the ship he worked on, The Eksund, I think it was called, or something like that, was used to carry the biggest haul of weapons the IRA had ever tried to smuggle into Ireland, and it's capture, some time after I was due to meet the skipper, marked the moment when the powers that be realised the IRA had the finances and contacts to raise and equip what amounted to an army.'

'Blimey!'

'Maybe the Libyans or perhaps the IRA caught up with Eoin O'Grady, and maybe it was he who betrayed the gun runners. I guess we will never know, but I think we should cover this, and my previous involvement in the past may create a good story with some solid background.'

'Absolutely. I see your point, Auntie Caroline.'

'You will need to get in touch with the Irish Police and perhaps chat up the Coastguard and the person who found the body to start digging on this one, Bobbie.'

'I'm on it,' said Bobbie, as a thrill of excitement ran up her spine. She was in for a busy week.

-oo0Ooo-

'Well, then you will have to go there in person' Caroline was saying. 'How far away is this Ballybunion place?'

Bobbie explained where Ballybunion was, that she had established that the hotel on the golf links adjacent to where the body was discovered had a room at a reasonable price, and that she could fly into an airport not too far away with a budget airline.

'Ballybunion sounds a pretty unlikely name to me,' said Caroline. 'Are you sure its genuine?'

'Yes. I've checked it out. I've found out it is on what is called the 'Wild Atlantic Way,' which is a popular tourist thing, and the body was on a little beach just outside the town. The people from the hotel know the woman who found it and put me in touch, and she seems quite happy to meet me.'

'Well done, Bobbie. Better get down there as soon as you can before the press pack descends.'

'Will you be all right?'

'Of course. As it happens, I've got to go over to the hospital tomorrow again, and they might want to keep me in for what they call "observation" overnight, probably because they can't believe how well I'm feeling, so I will be well cared for.'

'Well, if you are sure …'

-oo0Ooo-

Kerry Airport is 37.5kms from Ballybunion, and Ryanair deposited Bobbie on time at the terminal, where the cheapest hire car she could find on the internet would be waiting to take her to the hotel by the golf links.

A small dark-haired man was waiting in the arrivals area to meet her, holding up a crumpled envelope with her name on it.

'Hello. I'm Declan ' he said as she made herself known to him. 'If you would like to follow me, I'll take you to your car.'

They walked past the desks of several of the better-known car hire companies and then out into the 'Drop Off ' area, where people were loading and unloading passengers and luggage.

She was surprised to see that the car Declan approached was quite dirty and obviously not new.

'Is this the car? 'she asked.

'Well, bless you, no!' stated the little man. 'There is no room to park here at the airport, so we just pick people up here and take them to the office. It's just you today, so we can get straight off, if you are ready. We are not like these big companies with desks here; that is how we keep our prices down. I took your booking on the internet myself, by the way.'

-ooOOoo-

Bobbie had driven a little Hyundai similar to the one she drove now once before, in Spain, and she recognised the way it seemed to hop about and the distinctive, busy clattering engine note. It seemed this one was an earlier model and was obviously well used.

It rattled its way to her destination well enough, however, as she pulled up outside Pauline Patrick's little cottage in good time for their appointment. And to the accompaniment of a small dog barking within, she rang the doorbell.

'I knew you had booked into the hotel. Is everything all right there?' Mrs Patrick said as she opened the door.

This rather unexpected opening line caught Bobbie off guard a little.

'Er, yes. Thank you … why did you …'

'Oh, sorry,' said Pauline as she ushered Bobbie into the little sitting room. 'I suppose you would say it is taking a proprietorial interest … you see my husband used to own that hotel and left it to me when he passed away.'

Bobbie noticed that, despite her Irish-sounding name, her host spoke with a slightly clipped Surrey accent.

'Have you lived here long, Mrs Patrick?' asked Bobbie.

'About a year, and call me Pauline, please. And accept my apologies for asking about the hotel, you must think me very strange. It's just that since I found that dead body, I seem to be all at sixes and sevens somehow.'

'I imagine it was a considerable shock. What did you do when you came across it?'

'Well, the first thing was to try to get Buster here to leave it alone. The little rascal had slipped his collar and was pawing at it as I tried to get him back under control. Pauline reached down and patted the little dog as she spoke. 'Would you like some tea?'

'No, thank you, I had a coffee at the hotel, but don't let me stop you … So what did you do?'

'Well, I called the police, and they told me to stay put, so I had to wait by the body until they arrived with the coastguard people. I can't say that was a pleasant experience, and the body had obviously been in the water some time.'

'I'm told the hands and feet were tied together?'

'Yes, and behind the poor man's back, so that he was tied into a sort of kneeling position with his wrists and ankles tightly bound with thin blue nylon rope. You could see it was tight because it had cut into the flesh around the ankles where his trousers had ridden up a bit. There was no blood, of course. He had been in the water too long for that, although the body was not yet bloated, probably because the sea was quite cold.'

'Revolting, and an unpleasant experience for you, having to wait with the body.'

'Funnily enough, it didn't smell, so he can't have been dead that long, but it was not an experience I should like to repeat in a hurry.'

'I can well imagine. So when the police arrived, what did you do?'

'Well, it was only young Shaun and his Sergeant from the local station, and until the coastguard people got there, I'm not sure they knew what to do. Shortly after that, though, an ambulance arrived and a chap from the … the Irish Times, I think it was, turned up and started taking photographs. They seemed very professional, as if this sort of thing was commonplace for them.'

'The Irish Times, you say?'

'Yes.'

'Well, it is very kind of you to agree to see me, Pauline, and I do realise that the press can be a bit intrusive.'

'Not at all, he was the only one I've seen apart from you, and he told me that it was only because he was here to play golf that he got involved at all.'

'Well, I confess I'm a bit surprised at that. It can't be every day a body washes up on the beach with a bullet hole in the head …'

To read on, check out Bob Able books on Amazon!

To find more of Bob Able's books on Amazon … Follow this link:- https://www.amazon.co.uk/stores/Bob-Able/author/B07VZBFFBZ

Or enter 'Bob Able books' on Google or to search the Amazon bookstore.

Disclaimer:

Note: All rights reserved. No part of this book, ebook, manuscript or associated published or unpublished works may be copied, reproduced or transmitted by any means, electronic, mechanical, photocopying or otherwise, without the prior written permission of the author.

Copyright: Bob Able 2026

The author asserts the moral right under the Copyright, Design and Patents Act 1988 to be identified as the author of this work.
This is a work of fiction. Any similarities between any persons, living or dead and the characters in this work are purely coincidental.
The author accepts no claims in relation to this work.

Printed in Dunstable, United Kingdom